CASUALTY REPORT

ed vega

Arte Publico Press
Houston
Texas
1991

;rant from the National Endowment

The following stories first appeared in these publications: "Peso Mosca," *Nuestro*, August 1981. "Spanish Roulette," *Revista Chicano-Riqueña*, Vol. VII, No. 2, Spring 1980. "An Apology to the Moon Furies," *Hispanics in the United States: An Anthology of Creative Literature*, eds. Gary D. Keller and Francisco Jimenez. Ypsilanti, Michigan: Bilingual Press, 1980. "The Kite," *Revista Chicano-Riqueña*, Vol. VIII, No. 1, Winter 1980. "Horns," *Nuestro*, August 1979. "Fishing," *Nuestro*, June 1978. "Wild Horses," *Nuestro*, July 1977.

Arte Publico Press
University of Houston
Houston, Texas 77204-2090

Cover Design by Mark Piñón
Original painting by Simón Guss García:
"Eroding Image," Copyright © 1987

Vega, Ed, 1938–
        Casualty Report / Ed Vega.
            p.   cm.
        ISBN 1-55885-034-1
        I. Title.
    PS3572.E34C37 1991
    813'.54–dc20   91-7868
                                                                      CIP

The paper used in this publication meets the minimum requirements of the American National Standard for Permanence of Paper for Printed Library Materials Z39.48-1984. ∞

This book is dedicated to the memory of Alberto Vega Lebrón, my father, a kind and gentle man.

MINORITY POEM

Epileptically he shook
As if every organ in his body had exploded
Blood splattered as he spoke

Yet his hand held on to the gun
Aimed at the man alone in his suit
Reading *The New York Times.*

Take it back, he said, take it all back,
Turning the gun toward himself,
Or so help me, I'm warning you, I swear.

Julio Marzán
—Translations Without Originals

CONTENTS

Casualty Report

HORNS

Far away, in the distance of time created by memories, little has changed. I can still hear the screams pierce the gentle lulling of the night and see the colors of morning and hear its sounds. The sky was always blue except when it rained and then it didn't matter because Mercedes and I went outside and ran around the house, splashing in the mud. Round and round we went, laughing and talking nonsense, holding our mouths open to drink the rain and stopping only to pick up mangoes and guavas knocked down by the wind. When we got tired of running and eating wet fruit, we went under the big house supported by thick, high posts and sat with the goats and watched the rain march in straight lines, falling and making rivers on the black earth. Sometimes we sailed matchstick boats on the rivers made by the rain.

The woman screamed a long time and the man sounded as if he were being choked by his anger. When the screaming stopped we heard people shouting that the man had a knife. The murder took place one night as Mercedes and I were being put to bed by Grandma. The next day *El Imparcial* carried a front page picture of the dead woman lying on the floor, the front of her dress black from the blood. The man, his head down and his hands manacled at his belt, stood seemingly numbed by his regret, at the dead woman's feet. There was a policeman on each side of the man. The headlines in the newspaper read: POR CELOS CONCUBINA RECIBE 47 PUÑALADAS (BECAUSE OF JEALOUSY CONCUBINE IS STABBED 47 TIMES).

The screaming brought back memories of the previous year when Pedrito died. That morning it was Pedrito's mother who screamed. His death was an accident and I lay in bed, hearing both women, one now and the other then, listening to the night beyond the screaming, my body traveling far away from the terror. In the night the owl called. High in the tamarind tree it called.

Gloria my aunt came into the room and said it was the woman in the alley. Poor woman, she said, and Grandma said, Dear God. In the dimly lit room Gloria my aunt appeared luminous, her skin so white. Mercedes came in out of her own room and wanted to know if Grandpa was getting his gun and Grandma said for

11

Mercedes to get up on the bed with me, but Mercedes protested and Grandma picked her up and put her on the end of the bed, against the wall. Abuela crossed herself once more and spoke to Gloria my aunt in a whisper.

Stay with them, she said.

And Gloria my aunt, smelling of Maja soap, her black hair blending with the night from the window behind her, sat on the bed. Only her lips smiled and she spoke very softly and said that Mercedes and I must not be frightened. Mercedes attempted to speak several times, but Gloria my aunt said sssh. She put a finger to her lips and stroked Mercedes' hair.

We must be very quiet, she said.

Mercedes wanted to know why.

We must, please, Gloria my aunt said.

The owl called again and I listened trying to understand.

It was the woman in the alley, wasn't it, Titi Gloria, Mercedes said.

I think so, but don't think about it, Gloria my aunt said.

Maybe Grandpa will shoot somebody, Mercedes said.

I said that our uncle Roberto also had a gun because he had been in the war, but I didn't know if this was true and was only trying to keep up with Mercedes.

Once more Gloria my aunt said we must be very quiet and that if we were good she would tell us a story. We both nodded and Gloria my aunt began telling us about the pirate Cofresí. After a while, when the screaming was over and the voices died down, Grandma returned to the room and said she had made hot chocolate. We came out of the bedroom in our pajamas and sat at the dining room table and drank sweet, milky chocolate from the blue and white cups with Chinese pagodas on them. Abuela gave us soda crackers with butter and guava preserves to eat with the chocolate. When Grandpa returned he would not say much other than to confirm that it was the woman in the alley. Mercedes began to ask about the gun, but Grandpa looked at her once and she was quiet.

In the morning, after Grandpa had finished his breakfast and gone down into the yard and into his kiosk to begin work, Mercedes and I looked at the newspaper and tried counting the stab wounds on the body in the photograph but could only find twelve and not forty-seven as the headline said. We looked at the comics and we argued about Trucutrú. I tore part of the newspaper but Grandpa did not find out. In the afternoon Mercedes and I went to buy salt for Grandma and stopped at the little house in the alleyway where the murder took place. There were dark bloodstains on the unpainted, weatherbeaten walls of the porch. I asked Mercedes why the man had killed the woman and she said it happened because the woman was his concubine. I did not understand but Mercedes would go no further with her explanation. Instead, she gave me a look of disdain at my lack of sophistication.

When we were back in the house I read the newspaper story again, but understood little more than the first time. The man, who was married and lived in Río Piedras, had seen his concubine talking to another man earlier in the day.

When he arrived at her house that evening the man and the woman had argued and he had killed her.

That evening, as the sun began to set and the air took on its purplish glow and the wind shifted to bring the salt air from the sea, I asked Grandpa to explain the word concubine. As if he had not heard me speak, Grandpa walked away, returned with his razor strop and, with a fury which up to that time I had only suspected, hit me once across the back of the legs. I ran away crying and hid under the house until nightfall when I could only see the intermittent green light of the fireflies in the air.

With my back against one of the posts supporting the house I attempted to drown myself in sorrow, but instead found myself hypnotized by the cool, velvety softness of the night. Like a piece of music one has heard repeatedly and taken for granted only to be awakened one day to its beauty, I listened intently to each delicate sound: crickets, frogs, bats chirping as they hunted moths; the insistent, melancholic two-tone cry of the fragile *coquí*, and high in the tamarind tree, the owl, its call long and mournful. Further away, perhaps in that part of the mind which constructs the future, I heard the ocean crashing against some distant shore and for the first time knew I was a prisoner and wanted to be free. When Mercedes came to call me for supper I informed her that I was going away.

Tonight? she said derisively.

Tomorrow, I answered. I'm going to the lagoon and steal a boat. I'll sail far away and never come back.

Mercedes laughed and said I was being silly.

They'll find you and it'll be worse. They'll send you back to Cacimar.

I don't care, I said.

What will you eat?

I'll fish for shrimp.

Maybe you'll drown and the shrimp will eat you.

I did not answer and Mercedes said I should come and eat and that Saturday Gloria my aunt was taking us to the movies. I shrugged off the bribe and she went away. Above, on the porch of the house, I heard her tell Grandma that I was under the house, pouting—*tiene la trompa como un elefante*—explaining that my resentment was such that my mouth resembled an elephant's trunk. Our grandmother scolded Mercedes and said she shouldn't talk that way because she wasn't yet grown up. Finally, driven by a combination of my hunger and the mosquitoes, I came out from under the house.

No one said anything about my self-imposed exile. Abuela had cooked *bacalao con papas*, yellow rice mixed with white beans, and *tortitas de maíz*. The codfish was a little too salty but the corn fritters were good and I had eight. Four were sweet and the others not. After supper Grandma gave us ice cream made from goat's milk, mixed with sugar and cinnamon. Mercedes said it tasted like snow and then the two of us got into an argument since I felt there was no way Mercedes could know this. She said she did because her mother had described snow in a letter, and that if I knew anything about anything I would recognize that snow was sweet because as it fell it picked up nectar from the flowers. There was no arguing with Mercedes and I returned to my plan for running away.

At seven o'clock, as was his nightly habit, Grandpa turned on the radio in the living room and listened to the news with our uncle Roberto. Our other uncle, Marcial, was at the other end of the house, studying. Roberto had fought in Germany and Italy during the war and still used a cane because of his wounds. The war had been over almost two weeks but news of the invasion of Japan continued to pour in. The newscaster sounded like the same one who did the baseball games. Instead of flyballs falling in the outfield, however, he talked excitedly about the effects of the atomic bombs that had fallen somewhere in Japan. When the newscaster finished the war news and began talking about less exciting things, Mercedes went to her room and brought back the new book her mother had sent her from New York. The book, *El Conde de Montecristo*, had been printed in Barcelona. We went through the color illustrations in the leatherbound volume and then Mercedes began reading out loud. We were out on the porch and as I looked inside the living room the light from the dim light bulb above Grandpa made his shadow, as he hunched closer to the radio, look like that of the devil. The shadow extended all the way up the living room walls, making the head of the devil and its horns bend crazily up on the rafters. Down the street a dog howled and Mercedes stopped reading. We stopped rocking on the porch swing and listened.

He smells the blood, Mercedes said knowingly. Who? I said.

The dog, silly. They get wild when they smell human blood. The smell makes them turn into wolves and they start calling other dogs to join the pack.

I asked why.

To hunt people, Mercedes said with confidence.

I had never heard of this but I considered it a possibility.

And they turn into wolves? I said.

Yes, Gabriel, into wolves with long hair and very sharp teeth.

And they eat people?

Of course they eat people. It's impossible to turn the wolves back into dogs again. They have to be caught and poisoned. I read it in a history book.

No, you didn't, I said, suddenly feeling violated by her insistence.

All right, don't believe me. Go out there and see.

Maybe I will, I said.

Go ahead. Let them rip out your kidneys so you can't breathe.

I reconsidered and asked her if the dogs really turned into wolves.

Yes, she said, of course they do.

I looked over at Sentinel resting at Grandpa's feet, but the howling didn't seem to be affecting him. Sentinel, perhaps because of his large size and ferocious appearance, was rarely given to emotional outbursts. He was a good watchdog, however, and went with me whenever I went to the lagoon. Up to that time he had figured prominently in my escape plans. The more I thought about leaving, however, the weaker my resolve grew. The prospect of being hunted down by a pack of wolves finally settled the matter. That wolves were unheard of on the island, except in imported literature and films, did not lessen my fear.

Mercedes resumed reading. Once again we began rocking the porch swing and I soon fell asleep. The following night Mercedes refused to get her book and said I was an *ingrato*. I thought she was calling me a cat and we had another argument about who looked more like a cat. Grandpa settled the matter by reminding us that unless we stopped bickering we would both look like toasted bread, his current euphemism for a dose of his razor strop.

On Saturday Gloria my aunt made us take showers, dress up, put on shoes and socks and comb our hair neatly. Mercedes wore yellow ribbons on the ends of her pigtails. We took a bus to Río Piedras, changed to the San Juan bus and went to the movies. For me, who had never been inside a theater before that summer, the air-conditioning smelled wonderfully sweet and the plush seats seemed like kingly thrones. I shivered from the excitement and Mercedes quickly informed me that I would never be able to live in the United States since it was always cold there. She had never been to *el extranjero*, as all adults called that magical land, but her mother's letters, which Mercedes kept locked in a carved wooden jewelry box, would no doubt have supported her argument. I had no choice but to believe her. More to the point, the contents of her small treasure chest were, according to her, as sacred as the Gospel, since they contained *el amor de una madre ausente*, the love of an absent mother. That this phrase was usually reserved for Mother's Day and carried with it the connotation of not an absent mother, but a deceased one, was lost on Mercedes. Mercedes' mother, my aunt Teresa, was very much alive and teaching Spanish at a small college in New York. In spite of my shortcomings as a potential *yanqui*, I became accustomed to the air conditioning and thoroughly enjoyed the film. We saw an Errol Flynn swashbuckler and afterwards I decided to pursue a career in piracy when I grew up.

Gloria my aunt sat us in front and then returned to the back of the theater with the slight, blond-haired young man who had been waiting for us in the lobby of the theater. Before going beyond the curtains, Gloria my aunt had pulled Mercedes and me aside and made us promise not to tell anyone about Tony, explaining that he was an American friend from the university. If we told, she wouldn't be able to bring us to the movies again. I asked why and Mercedes pinched my arm. Gloria my aunt said we really had to promise, so we both touched a cross made from thumb and index finger to our lips and swore on our mothers.

The next day Mercedes explained the mystery.

They're lovers, stupid! she said.

Is he bad? I asked perplexed by her remark.

Of course not, Mercedes said, placing both fists on her hips and closing her eyes in desperation.

And she loves him? I said.

Yes.

But she's married.

That's the way it's supposed to be. The woman has to keep it a secret. It's like that in all the *novelas* on the radio.

But why?

Because! said Mercedes. You ask so many stupid questions that sometimes I wonder if we're really cousins, Gabriel.

I don't care if we are or not and I don't believe you about Titi Gloria. I'm going to ask Grandma. She listens to all the *novelas*.

We were standing by the front gate, picking at the red hibiscus blossoms and watching the humming birds as they went from flower to flower. It was Sunday and Gloria my aunt was taking us to church in Rio Piedras. The sun was already quite hot and I felt uncomfortable dressed all in white. Any slight movement might bring a stain or a smudge to my clothing. My short pants were too tight and my habit of placing one foot on top of the other threatened to ruin the white sheen of my shoes. I began to develop a headache and an extreme dislike for the shoes.

In the kiosk next to the house Grandpa was working on someone's shoes, the striking of hammer upon anvil making a drumming sound on the leather. Usually a rhythmic sound, the pounding now added to the throbbing in my head and I again threatened to ask Grandma about lovers. Mercedes pulled me away from the fence and around the side of the house. Standing near the shower stall under the tamarind tree, she warned me about being a *lengüilargo*, a long-tongue or tattletale—the word was a favorite in her adult repertoire of admonitory terms. At the age of nine it was easy for me to imagine a ribbon of tongue, hanging from one's mouth and reaching down to the belt buckle like my father's ties. As if I had been suddenly poked in the ribs, I dissolved into uncontrollable laughter.

You better stop right now, Gabrielito, Mercedes said sternly. If Grandpa hears you, he's going to ask questions.

So! I'll tell him and then we'll see who's telling the truth.

You wouldn't dare.

Yes, I would.

Oh, please, Gabriel. If you tell him about Tony, Titi Gloria's life will be ruined.

Why, because he's American?

No, you idiot, because they're lovers! *Amantes*. You promised not to tell. You swore on Titi Marta and I on my mother. ¡*Ay, Dios Santo*! There will be a tragedy. *Una tragedia*. You promised, Gabriel!

I was not moved by Mercedes' urgency but before I could utter another word, Gloria my aunt was calling us to hurry. I took off running and was already holding our aunt's hand when Mercedes, fuming, turned the corner of the house. I often thought that I loved my aunt more than my mother, but knew it wasn't true and that my love for her was different. Gloria Ocasio de Torres was always smiling, sang beautifully and never raised her voice in anger. She wrote poetry and her large green eyes shimmered liquidly like the wings of a humming-bird. Wherever she went men always said wonderful things about her—strange things about dew upon rose petals, heaven, wounded hearts and doves without nests. Mercedes said these words were *piropos*, gifts offered to a woman's beauty by her admirers. Gifts or not, the words didn't seem to affect Gloria my aunt. Niece and nephew held firmly by the hand and head held high, she passed among the men like a summery ocean breeze, strong, yet pleasing.

I didn't understand much about people being lovers but suspected it was close to being a sin. In church that morning I asked God to forgive Gloria my aunt. On the way back from town it rained heavily. Sitting on the bus amusing myself by watching the steady rain and wiggling my toes inside my soaked and muddied shoes, I happened to look up and see my aunt lost in thought and apparently saddened by the rain.

Another week went by and each time I looked at my aunt she appeared sadder and now would remain in her room, shaded by the tamarind tree, staring out of the window at the mountains to the east. Mercedes said it was because the war was over and Aníbal, Gloria's husband, was returning and because her summer classes at the university were over and she couldn't see Tony anymore. Again Mercedes mentioned tragedy. I asked her what she meant but Mercedes rolled her eyes up into her head and looked at me as if I couldn't possibly understand.

To prove that being a year older than me didn't make her that much wiser, I told Mercedes that my friends had told me the meaning of the word concubine. When I explained, Mercedes said I was lying and that no woman would ever do anything like that, especially down there where babies came from, and that if I didn't stop she was going to tell Grandpa. I took it all back and said I had made everything up.

Another week went by and quite suddenly things began happening very quickly. The speckled hen hatched eleven chicks, Mercedes cut her finger on the front gate, our uncle, Roberto, announced that he was seeing a young woman and had already spoken to her father and that he would enroll in the university for the fall semester to study law; our other uncle, Marcial, received all A's in his summer studies. My parents wrote to say that they would be coming soon, but when Grandma told me this she appeared concerned and distant. A heaviness suddenly had taken over and I couldn't figure out why.

The only happy occasion was Aníbal's homecoming. One morning about an hour after we had finished eating breakfast, Aníbal walked in looking quite handsome and serious in his corporal's uniform. On his shoulder he wore the red and yellow patch of the 65th Infantry Regiment with the outline of El Morro Castle. Like Roberto, Aníbal had also been wounded in combat and wore two rows of battle ribbons on his chest. As if to prove his conquest of the enemy Aníbal presented Grandpa, Martín Ocasio, his father-in-law, an iron cross. Aníbal said it had belonged to a German general. As solemnly as if he were accepting the enemy's surrender, Grandpa accepted the medal, shook hands with his son-in-law and then embraced him stiffly.

Gloria my aunt emerged from her misery and appeared happy for the first time in weeks. She cried and laughed when she first saw Aníbal, and every time she was with him clung desperately to his arm. There was, it seemed to me, a quiet sadness to Gloria my aunt. Whenever I sought her out she appeared distracted and would answer my questions with a listlessness that made me worry. Two days later she and Aníbal left for their new home on the other side of the island.

That afternoon I went to the lagoon with my friends. The subject of the murder in the alley came up again. One after the other, my friends imitated the woman's screams. Fafo, who at twelve was the oldest and appeared to me to know everything there was to know about such matters, said the woman deserved what she got.

Her husband stabbed her forty-seven times. One for each of the horns she put on his head.

I tried to tell them that the man wasn't her husband, but no one would listen. Everyone was laughing and eventually I joined in. Like naked goats we ran back and forth, stabbing each other with fingers held to our foreheads. *Cabrón* ... *cabrón* ... *cabrón* ... we yelled as we pranced around the grassy sand dunes near the lagoon.

After a while, exhausted, I put on my clothes and sat down on the shore. On the far coast of the lagoon, everything in miniature, three fishermen were dragging a large net in the blue water, the sun glinting gold on their brown backs. Down the beach, where the palm trees grew bowed to the trade winds and the wire fence extended 50 feet out into the water to make the country club private, six men were practicing their skeet shooting, the puffs of dark smoke from the clay pigeons visible before one heard the muffled sound of the shotguns. I walked through the white sand, listening to the wind in the palms, until I was near the fence. Tony, my aunt's friend, was with the other men, smiling and talking in English, his blond hair carelessly blowing in the wind. It all came together then, and like a fast-moving storm cloud which suddenly turns the air dark, a deep grieving, deeper than I had felt at the loss of my friend Pedrito, settled over me and I was overcome with remorse and fear for my aunt's life.

I turned back and walked along the water's edge, watching the small waves lapping at the sand and far away the fishermen casting their net. The sky was blue and very high, a few small clouds, white and fluffy drifting below. My friends were now swimming or resting on the sand but I didn't go near them. I cut through the acerola bushes until I found the road and walked on one of the ruts made by the cars that went to the country club, my head down and tears wanting to come, but only feeling the tightness in my throat so that I thought I would never cry again.

Now my parents would come and I would have to return to Cacimar and school to endure the taunts of the others and Pedrito would not be there to help me. He was gone and there would be no more private jokes or serious conversations about building bridges and I'd finally have to fight the big Andino boy because he wouldn't stop talking about my curly hair and why I didn't wear ribbons in it.

That night I remained awake until quite late and heard the owl calling, sad and deep calls, but I didn't know what it meant. Three days later my parents arrived. My father brought me a Chinese checkers game and my mother hugged me so hard that I couldn't stop laughing, but the sadness would not go away. Abuela had Roberto kill a fat red hen and she made soup and *arroz con gallina* and for dessert she made *flan*. I helped beat the egg yolks until my arm hurt and I wondered if I would be able to pitch again. That night I slept between my father and mother and did not hear the owl.

In the morning, after breakfast my father and mother asked me to come out on the porch and we sat down in chairs and my father explained that the family would be moving to the United States, but that my sister and I would remain behind for a year or so; my sister with a cousin of his in Guayama and I with my grandparents there in Laguna Seca. I shook my head but no words would come out and finally I ran to my mother and buried my head on her shoulder, wanting to cry but not able to. My father said it would only be for a short time until he and my mother could find a place to live and that I had to be brave. My mother said all my clothes and toys would be coming the following week and that she loved me very much. I told her that I loved her too, but I was lying. I felt nothing.

When we sat down to eat lunch my father and mother talked about their plans and my father talked about opening up a shoe store and what a good business that would be because people in the Spanish-speaking community, which was growing, would need different types of shoes for different seasons, especially in the winter and that now that the war was over rubber would be available again. My mother said that perhaps they could also sell umbrellas and raincoats. Grandpa was pleased about the shoe business but didn't like the idea of mixing in raincoats and umbrellas. He shot my mother a stern look but my mother smiled sweetly at him and said that perhaps they could send him orders for shoes to be custom-made or perhaps he could make standard sizes and they could sell them in their new store.

Grandpa nodded several times but everyone knew he didn't like the idea. No one mentioned Gloria my aunt except that my mother asked how she was and Grandma said she was fine and that she and Aníbal were happy. I didn't believe any of them. I hated them and knew they were lying. That afternoon my father and mother said goodbye and left. They both kissed me and my mother said again that she loved me. I didn't say anything and she asked me, tears in her eyes, if I didn't love her.

I love you, I said, but the words had no meaning.

I swore to myself I would never love anyone again, even if it meant breaking my promise to marry Pedrito's sister. Thinking about it all made everything inside of me hurt. I knew even then that I was being held captive by them and that if I let myself, I would cry.

WILD HORSES

From the moment the plan came to Amalia Santiago she wished for a miracle. Nothing had gone right that month. The check wasn't due for another week, Don Miguel at the *bodega* had refused her further credit and she was too proud to call Pete. They were his children too, but that didn't matter to him. Numbers clicked inside Amalia's head as if her brain were an adding machine. Not a day passed when the three-digit number didn't appear. Clear, exact, turning up sometimes in a dream, sometimes in the street. ... An address, the price of an item in a store, the number offered Amalia a measure of hope. Now, as she made ready to leave, the numbers came only randomly: a bill to pay, an obligation to fulfill. It had been wrong to buy the crib for Lourdes' baby.

It had finally come, she thought. 3 4 7! After letting the number fly around the room a few times to test it, it returned to her as a bird to its nest. She tried changing the numbers, matching them as one would do with articles of clothing. She had never been surer. Amalia weighed the pros and cons of the gamble for several minutes. In the end, knowing as one does when a cause is lost, she decided against it. It had been months since she had last hit so that her plan became the only alternative. To play the little money she had seemed a great risk.

Amalia put on her coat, let herself out of the apartment, and began the tiresome six-flight descent to the street. It always seemed more difficult to go down the stairs, since she would eventually have to return. Grasping the staircase railing as if it were her lifeline to safety, she fought the stench of urine emanating from the stairwell. On the third floor someone had broken open a bag of garbage, and its contents, a mosaic of rice, beans, half-eaten *tostones* and stripped-clean pork chop bones, stared back at her sullenly. She didn't care. If they wanted to be pigs, let them. Even the strange, thick scrawlings on the walls seemed natural. Who cared if they sprayed their names and made the building look as if hippies lived in it. What she was about to do was far lower on the scale of values she had learned while growing up on the island.

All of it was punishment, she thought as she reached the ground floor. Pete going off with the woman from the Bronx right after Lissette was born, Tony's asthma, Lourdes getting pregnant a year after finishing junior high, not getting into the projects, and being refused the job as teacher's aide because of her treatment at St. Luke's Hospital were all part of the punishment. Who wouldn't go crazy with six kids to raise? She had done nothing to deserve it. She was a good mother. After Pete left she hadn't let another man into the house.

As she walked she hoped for a short line at the supermarket. Her feet hurt but she laughed painfully at the irony of the situation. Pete had promised Bobby a Husky for his twelfth birthday. That had come and gone without Pete even showing up. She was sure there would be a line. But there had always been lines: checks to be cashed, food stamps to purchase, mail to be called for at the post office. Nothing was safe from the junkies if left in the mailbox. And waiting rooms. Her life was filled with thoughts which, like the rising morning woodsmoke of her mountain childhood, had come to her in waiting rooms: prenatal care, infant care, dental clinics, emergency rooms, school registration, investigators to see. The thoughts flowed like a never-ending dream, no one thought linked to another, but more like strangers passing each other on a crowded street. Sometimes there had been thoughts of houses with warm quiet rooms with thick carpeting and bright pictures on the walls, rooms where laughter came across to her like the tinkling of fine crystal and everything happened slowly, ever so slowly, so that it was like watching a beautiful love story on film. She was then transported to other places, new cities and towns, where people addressed each other politely and if they were unhappy they sang songs, silly songs with little meaning. And she saw the men, strong and brave men who never threatened or lied or raised their voices in anger, good men who loved their children and their home. Gina's comadre had said Pete was supporting the other woman's children.

Amalia tried to make her mind blank but the thoughts still came. She walked across Amsterdam Avenue to Broadway, began crossing the street to the super-market and changed her mind. She was bound to run into someone and she'd have to explain: "I'm buying it for Doña Jacinta. *Sí, la pobrecita. Sí, bendito.* Her arthritis is acting up again, you know. Her dog's going to have puppies and you know how they get when they're pregnant."

Nobody would believe her. In any case the young Dominican girls at the checkout counters would talk. God, how they gossiped and joked! They loved it when a Puerto Rican ran into bad luck. But that wasn't it. Even her own, the ones with men, relished her misfortune. Six years and not one man had touched her. Amalia didn't want to think about it any more. She'd have to walk to the 80s where nobody knew her.

Amalia made the trip there and back, her stomach aching, not feeling the deeper pain, which had turned to stone long ago. The few coins in her coat pocket had jingled as she walked and each time she passed a pizza shop she'd had to fight the urge to spend the money. Instead, she had made herself window-shop, stopping every so often to price the items for the children. Christmas was still several months away but she made herself think of elaborate strategies for getting toys into the apartment and hiding them. And she watched the people in the street, the white mothers pushing baby carriages, the babies fat-faced and pink in the cold air. A baby carriage, rather than a crib, would have been more practical.

When she finally got back to the apartment, Amalia collapsed on the worn couch in the living room. She fixed her eyes on the brick wall beyond the kitchen window. Her energies sapped from fighting the stairs, it suddenly seemed to her that she had never noticed how close the wall was to her own window. It almost appeared as if in her absence someone had moved the two buildings closer together. As she focused her eyes she realized the distance was the same. Nothing had changed on that wall. Ten years and nothing had changed. The brick, year in and year out, was the same hen-colored red.

After a while Amalia stood up, removed her coat and looked at herself in the faded mirror on the wall above the cracked fish tank she'd bought her children two years before. The sand was covered with a fine film of dust and the plastic plants were doubly lifeless in repose. She seemed to herself thinner than ever, paler. Her hair, her once-thick black hair, hung like dark rain on each side of her gaunt face. She drew closer and, examining herself for gray hairs, pulled one out. Looking at it for a moment as if mourning her faded youth, Amalia smiled sadly at herself and let the silver strand float through the sunlight streaming in below the lowered shade on the window.

There would be no miracles, she thought. In another hour the children would be home from school. Her stomach felt queasy, much as if, within her, life had begun to stir anew. Eight times it had happened and six had survived. The other two had disappeared, had flown from her like tiny angels swathed in blood. *Dos santitos*, two little angels. A hundred candles and a thousand Hail Marys. She had cried then and the emptiness had been intense.

Kneeling in front of the kitchen sink and reaching behind it, Amalia retrieved the two empty cans she had hidden there the night before. The roaches hadn't gotten to them. She had wiped them clean after finding them in the garbage cans near Columbia University. Lost in the wonder of the new child and Lourdes' radiance, she'd almost missed them. The leaping, arched fish had intrigued her. *Arenque*, she'd thought. In her mind she saw the golden, smoked fish laid out in crates at the town store and images of her childhood in Cacimar flashed slowly before her eyes: the hot morning sun; the young, newly planted cane swaying gently in the afternoon breeze; rain falling steadily to make the earth rich with smells; and the *quebrada*, the small stream which traversed her world, swelling from the rain and roaring as it ran breakneck to the sea she'd never seen.

She'd placed the cans in the shopping bag and then, as she continued walking, resumed her train of thought concerning Lourdes and the baby. Her new station in life was still not quite believable. Thirty-five and already a grandmother. The new child had made Amalia momentarily happy but her feelings turned once more to the truth. In another two months he'd be another mouth to feed. *Comiendo y descomiendo*, eating and shitting, setting in motion once again the cycle of waiting rooms. And the father? If he was indeed the baby's father, conveniently out of harm's way on Riker's Island for drugs. Maybe he'd hang himself like Tata's cousin. She'd crossed herself against evil spirits and hurried on out of the shadows.

As she stood up, Amalia again wished she hadn't bought the crib. She placed the empty cans on the dinette table and with a single-edge razor, carefully removed their labels. When she was finished she took the ones she had purchased at the supermarket and ripped violently at the labels. She hated the alert, thick-tongued animal staring hungrily at her. Balling up the scraps of paper in her fist, she went to the window and raised it. A blast of cold air made her gasp. The act of disposing of the incriminating evidence produced a slight but short-lived feeling of satisfaction in Amalia.

Just as Dr. Kramer had said she must do with everything if she was to get well, Amalia had been able to proceed with the plan in steps. When she went to look for the glue, however, she couldn't find it. A wave of terror attacked her body and she nearly began sobbing. Her first thought was for Bobby. She immediately decided he was too smart. His models were his pride and joy and more than once she'd heard him complain that he enjoyed building them but hated the smell of glue. Bobby's dreams and his goodness made her feel stronger.

And then the panic struck once more, this time in a blinding, gray spasm which wracked her entire body. Perhaps he had run out of glue. There had to be some or the plan was ruined, her meager investment wasted. Dr. Kramer was right. She should always plan ahead. As the fear subsided Amalia thought about hunger and tried to understand it. Her stomach no longer hurt but she knew she was hungry because her head seemed lighter and somehow removed from the rest of her body, so that every time she stood up she had to protect herself against fainting. She couldn't recall when she had last eaten. Lourdes had offered her a dish of jello at the hospital but Amalia couldn't remember whether she had accepted it or urged the girl to finish her supper.

Fighting the nausea which now threatened to drown her, Amalia got down flat on the linoleum floor of the boys' room and searched under the bed until she found a second box where her son had placed the tube of glue. Slowly, as if she were walking in a dream, she returned to the kitchen and began replacing the labels. The nausea felt like a dry, empty room which spun slowly around inside of her. She worked carefully, fighting the dizzy spells. They came at her regularly now, as if a blanket were suddenly thrown over her to shut out the light.

She was an expert, she thought. How many plastic jewels had she set into brooches and pins back then when she worked at the factory and Pete couldn't keep his hands off her? Up on the roof, in the hall, in the movies he couldn't keep his hands off her, so that eventually they had to get married. Lourdes had arrived five months later. How many little jewels? How many fake diamonds?

How many stars? *¿Cuántas estrellas hay en el cielo?* She recalled the childhood riddle and its amusing answer. *Cincuenta.* Fifty. *Sin cuenta.* It made no sense in English. Without count. *Sin cuenta.* How many things couldn't be counted? As she worked Amalia tried making a list: grains of sand, of sugar, of rice, blades of grass, clouds, waves in the sea. Her mind wandered off and she thought of babies. Their mothers knew how many there were. *Sin cuenta.* Be careful, she told herself. *¡Ten cuenta!* Very careful. Just the right amount of glue and no wrinkles. Otherwise the children would suspect the truth.

When she was finished Amalia put the glue back exactly where Bobby had placed it in the box, returned the two finished cans to the cupboard and threw the empty cans out the window. She watched them hurtling earthward like silver projectiles until they crashed into the litter-filled backyard, the sound muffled by the accumulation of garbage which in summer sent draughts of sickly smells of putrefaction into the apartment. They'd understand someday, she thought.

Nothing much happened at dinner time, thought Amalia later that night. Exhausted, she lay in bed staring at the ceiling, Tony's heavy breathing on one side, his body frail, vulnerable, and Lissette's even smaller body snuggled against her. They had been good and only Bobby had been a little difficult. It was almost as if he had sensed the deception, but being brave, had kept the knowledge to himself. She had opened the cans and left them empty on the table for them to notice. Bobby had picked up one of the cans, smelled it suspiciously and informed the others that mackerel was similar to salmon. Tony and Emily, being younger, hadn't believed him. They insisted it was more like shark and turned the conversation into their own private joke about a recent movie, which they had not seen, but knew by heart.

"We're gonna get even with Jaws, right, Mami?"

Tony would be a joker just like his father, thought Amalia. Their laughter made her nervous but she'd hold on. The pills for her nerves had run out the day before. In any case they made her too sleepy. Amalia hadn't been sure about the family lineage of the mackerel but decided it was better if they kept busy talking and laughing. It was better than crying. She had never had any success in silencing them. The chore of preparing their supper had given her new energy. Once she finished she felt the listlessness again. There was a moment when Billy had balked at eating and made remarks about the texture of the meat, but he always complained and Amalia had to remember what Dr. Kramer had said about being in the middle. She hadn't understood all of it but it seemed to make sense. At the age of nine he couldn't decide whether to act like a little man and follow Bobby or act like Tony, who was seven.

Billy and Lissette had eaten everything on their plates and asked for seconds. Sitting atop the white mounds of rice, the meat looked no different from *carne vieja. Ropa vieja,* the Cubans called it. Old clothes. The onion, garlic and tomato sauce must have disguised the taste. She didn't know. She'd tried to eat but even with the hunger gnawing at her as if a beast were devouring itself from within, her stomach rebelled at the thought. It seemed, as she stared at her empty plate, as if she were involved in some innocent child's game in which friends had concocted an awful recipe and were daring her to try it. Her thoughts were broken when Emily spoke to her.

"Mami, you thinking about Papi again?"

"No, mamita. Don't worry. *No te apures.*"

"He's okay, right? He's gonna come back for my birthday, right?"

"Yes, honey. Yes, for your birthday."

And now, as Amalia lay in the darkness, forcing her eyes to close, she saw them. Beautiful wild horses, racing headlong into the wind, their manes like fire, their muscles straining and their nostrils flared wide. The sweat on their smooth brown skins glistened like fine wet leather. *Eso es criminal*, she thought, and wasn't sure whether her feelings were directed at the slaughtered animals or at the sacrilege she had committed.

The horses ran on and on in her mind until, unable to keep up with them, Amalia Santiago fell asleep.

Earlier that day, somewhere, somehow, hundreds of horses with colorfully dressed little men atop them and thousands of people cheering after having put their faith on them in green, sent half the population searching in back pages of newspaper where the truth of life was revealed: $1,417,347.

SPANISH ROULETTE

Sixto Andrade snapped the gun open and shut several times and then spun the cylinder, intrigued by the kaleidoscopic pattern made by the empty chambers. He was fascinated by the blue-black color of the metal, but more so by the almost toy-like quality of the small weapon. As the last rays of sunlight began their retreat from the four room tenement flat, Sixto once again snapped the cylinder open and began loading the gun. It pleased him that each brass and lead projectile fit easily into each one of the chambers and yet would not fall out. When he had finished inserting the last of the bullets, he again closed the cylinder and, enjoying the increased weight of the gun, pointed it at the ceiling and pulled back the hammer.

"What's the piece for, man?"

Sixto had become so absorbed in the gun that he did not hear Willie Collazo, with whom he shared the apartment, come in. His friend's question came at him suddenly, the words intruding into the world he had created since the previous weekend.

"Nothing," he said, lowering the weapon.

"What do you mean, 'nothing'?" said Willie. "You looked like you were ready to play Russian roulette when I came in, bro."

"No way, man," said Sixto, and as he had been shown by Tommy Ramos, he let the hammer fall back gently into place. "It's called Spanish roulette," he added, philosophically.

Willie's dark face broke into a wide grin and his eyes, just as if he were playing his congas, laughed before he did. "No kidding, man," he said. "You taking up a new line of work? I know things are rough but sticking up people and writing poetry don't go together."

Sixto put the gun on the table, tried to smile but couldn't, and recalled the last time he had read at the cafe on Sixth Street. Willie had played behind him, his hands making the drums sing a background to his words. "I gotta take care of some business, Willie," he said, solemnly, and, turning back to his friend, walked across the worn linoleum to the open window of the front room.

"Not like that, panita," Willie said as he followed him.

"Family stuff, bro."

"Who?"

"My sister," Sixto said without turning.

"Mandy?"

Sixto nodded, his small body taut with the anger he had felt when Mandy had finished telling him of the attack. He looked out over the street four flights below and fought an urge to jump. It was one solution but not *the* solution. Despairingly, he shook his head at the misery below: burned out buildings, torched by landlords because it was cheaper than fixing them; empty lots, overgrown with weeds and showing the ravages of life in the neighborhood. On the sidewalk, the discarded refrigerator still remained as a faceless sentinel standing guard over the lot, its door removed too late to save the little boy from Avenue B. He had been locked in it half the day while his mother, going crazy with worry, searched the streets so that by the time she saw the blue-faced child, she was too far gone to understand what it all meant.

He tried to cheer himself up by focusing his attention on the children playing in front of the open fire hydrant, but could not. The twilight rainbow within the stream of water, which they intermittently shot up in the air to make it cascade in a bright arc of white against the asphalt, was an illusion, *un engaño*, a poetic image of his childhood created solely to contrast his despair. He thought again of the crushed innocence on his sister's face and his blood felt like sand as it ran in his veins.

"You want to talk about it?" asked Willie.

"No, man," Sixto replied. "I don't."

Up the street, in front of the *bodega*, the old men were already playing dominoes and drinking beer. Sixto imagined them joking about each other's weaknesses, always, he thought ironically, with respect. They had no worries. Having lived a life of service to that which now beckoned him, they could afford to be light-hearted. It was as if he had been programmed early on for the task now facing him. He turned slowly, wiped an imaginary tear from his eyes and recalled his father's admonition about crying: "*Usted es un machito y los machos no lloran*, machos don't cry." How old had he been? Five or six, no more. He had fallen in the playground and cut his lip. His father's friends had laughed at the remark, but he couldn't stop crying and his father had shaken him. "*Le dije que usted no es una chancleta. ¡Apréndalo bien!*" "You are not a girl, understand that once and for all!"

Concerned with Sixto's mood, once again Willie tried drawing him out. "*Coño*, bro, she's only fifteen," he said. *¿Qué pasó?*"

The gentleness and calm which Sixto so much admired had faded from Willie's face and now mirrored his own anguish. It was wrong to involve his friend but perhaps that was part of it. Willie was there to test his resolve. He had been placed there by fate to make sure the crime did not go unpunished. In the end, when it came to act, he'd have only his wits and manhood.

"It's nothing, bro," Sixto replied, walking back into the kitchen. "I told you, family business. Don't worry about it."

"Man, don't be like that."

There was no injury in Willie's voice and as if someone had suddenly punched him in the stomach to obtain a confession, the words burst out of Sixto.

"*Un tipo la mangó en el rufo*, man. Some dude grabbed her. You happy now?"

"Where?" Willie asked, knowing that uttering the words was meaningless. "In the projects?"

"Yeah, last week. She got let out of school early and he grabbed her in the elevator and brought her up to the roof."

"And you kept it all in since you came back from your Mom's Sunday night?"

"What was I supposed to do, man? Go around broadcasting that my sister got took off?"

"I'm sorry, Sixto. You know I don't mean it like that."

"I know, man. I know."

"Did she know the guy? Un *cocolo*, right? A black dude. They're the ones that go for that stuff."

"No, man. It wasn't no *cocolo*."

"But she knew him."

"Yeah, you know. From seeing him around the block. *Un bonitillo*, man. Pretty dude that deals coke and has a couple of women hustling for him. A dude named Lino."

"*¿Bien blanco?* Pale dude with Indian hair like yours?"

"Yeah, that's the guy."

"Drives around in a gold Camaro, right?"

"Yeah, I think so." Willie nodded several times and then shook his head.

"He's Shorty Pardo's cousin, right?" Sixto knew about the family connection but hadn't wanted to admit it until now.

"So?" he said, defiantly.

"Those people are crazy, bro," said Willie.

"I know."

"They've been dealing *tecata* up there in El Barrio since forever, man. Even the Italians stay clear of them, they're so crazy."

"That doesn't mean nothing to me," said Sixto, feeling his street manhood, the bravado which everyone develops growing up in the street, surfacing. Bad talk was the antidote to fear and he wasn't immune to it. "I know how crazy they are, but I'm gonna tell you something. I don't care who the dude is. I'm gonna burn him. Gonna set his heart on fire with that piece."

"Hey, go easy, *panita*," said Willie. "Be cool, bro. I know how you feel but that ain't gonna solve nothing. You're an artist, man. You know that? A poet. And a playwright. You're gonna light up Broadway one of these days."

Willie was suddenly silent as he reflected on his words. He sat down on one of the kitchen chairs and lowered his head. After a few moments he looked up and said: "Forget what I said, man. I don't know what I'm talking about. I wouldn't know what to do if that happened to one of the women in my family. I probably would've done the dude in by now. I'm sorry I said anything. I just don't wanna see you messed up. And I'm not gonna tell you to go to the cops, either."

Sixto did not answer Willie. They both knew going to the police would serve no purpose. As soon as the old man found out, he'd beat her for not protecting herself. It would become a personal matter, as if it had been he who had submitted. He'd rant and rave about short skirts and lipstick and music and then compare everything to the way things were on the island and his precious hometown, his beloved Cacimar, like it was the center of the universe and the place where all the laws governing the human race had been created. But Sixto had nothing to worry about. He was different from his father. He was getting an education, had been enlightened to truth and beauty and knew about equality and justice. Hell, he was a new man, forged out of steel and concrete, not old banana leaves and coconuts. And yet he wanted to strike back and was sick to his stomach because he wanted Lino Quintana in front of him, on his knees, begging for mercy. He'd smoke a couple of joints and float back uptown to the Pardo's turf and then blast away at all of them like he was the Lone Ranger.

He laughed sarcastically at himself and thought that in the end he'd probably back down, allow the matter to work itself out and let Mandy live with the scar for the rest of her life. And he'd tell himself that rape was a common thing, even in families, and that people went on living and working and making babies like a bunch of zombies, like somebody's puppets without ever realizing who was pulling the strings. It was all crazy. You were born and tagged with a name: Rodríguez, Mercado, Torres, Cartagena, Pantoja, Maldonado, Sandoval, Ballester, Nieves, Carmona. All of them, funny-ass Spanish names. And then you were told to speak English and be cool because it was important to try and get over by imitating the Anglo-Saxon crap, since that's where all the money and success were to be found. Nobody actually came out and said it, but it was written clearly in everything you saw, printed boldly between the lines of books, television, movies, advertising. And at the place where you got your love, your mother's milk, your rice and beans, you were told to speak Spanish and be respectful and defend your honor and that of the women around you.

"I'm gonna burn him, Willie," Sixto repeated. "Gonna burn him right in his *güevos*. Burn him right there in his balls so he can feel the pain before I blow him away and let God deal with him. He'll understand, man, because I don't." Sixto felt the dizzying anger blind him for a moment. "*Coño*, man, she was just fifteen," he pleaded, as if Willie could absolve him of his sin before it had been committed. "I have to do it, man. She was just a kid. *Una nena*, man. A little innocent girl who dug Latin music and danced only with her girlfriends at home and believed all the nonsense about purity and virginity, man. And now this son of a bitch went and did it to her. *Le hizo el daño.*"

That's what women called it. The damage. And it was true. Damaged goods. He didn't want to believe it but that's how he felt. In all his educated, enlightened splendor, that's how he felt. Like she had been rendered untouchable, her femaleness soiled and smeared forever. Like no man would want to love her knowing what had happened. The whole thing was so devastating that he couldn't imagine what it was like to be a woman. If they felt even a little of what he was experiencing, it was too much. And he, her own brother, already talking as if she were dead. That's how bad it was. Like she was a memory.

"I'm gonna kill him, Willie," said Sixto once more, pounding on the wall. "*¡Lo mato, coño! Lo mato, lo mato,*" he repeated the death threat over and over in a frenzy. Willie stood up and reached for his arm but Sixto pulled roughly away. "It's cool, man," he said, and put his opened hands in front of him. "I'm all right. Everything's cool."

"Slow down," Willie pleaded. "Slow down."

"You're right, man. I gotta slow down." Sixto sat down but before long was up again. "Man, I couldn't sleep the last couple of nights. I kept seeing myself wearing the shame the rest of my life. I gave myself every excuse in the book. I even prayed, Willie. Me, a spic from the streets of the Big Apple, hip and slick, writing my *jíbaro* poetry; *saliéndome las palabras de las entrañas; inventando foquin mundos* like a god; like *foquin* Juracán pitching lightning bolts at the people to wake them from their stupor, man. Wake them up from their lethargy and their four hundred year old sleep of self-induced tyranny, you know?"

"I understand, man."

"Willie, man, I wanted my words to thunder, to shake the earth *pa' que la gente le pida a Yuquiyú que los salve.*"

"And it's gonna be that way, bro. You're the poet, man. The voice."

"And me praying. Praying, man. And not to Yuquiyú but to some distorted European idea. I'm messed up, bro. Really messed up. Writing all this jive poetry that's supposed to incite the people to take up arms against the oppressor and all the while my heart is dripping with feelings of love and brotherhood and peace like some programmed puppet, Willie."

"I hear you."

"I mean, I bought all that stuff, man. All that liberal American jive. I bought it. I marched against the war in Vietnam, against colonialism and capitalism, and for the Chicano brothers cracking their backs in the fields, marched till my feet were raw, and every time I saw lettuce or grapes, I saw poison. And man, it felt right, Willie."

"It was a righteous cause, man."

"And I marched for the independence of the island, of Puerto Rico, Willie: *de Portorro, de Borinquen, la buena, la sagrada, el terruño, madre de todos nosotros; bendita seas entre todas las mujeres y bendito sea el fruto de tu vientre pelú.* I marched for the land of our people and it felt right."

"It is right, man."

"You know, once and for all I had overcome all the anger of being a colonized person without a country and my culture being swallowed up, digested, and thrown back up so you can't even recognize what it's all about. I had overcome all the craziness and could stand above it; I could look down on the brothers and sisters who took up arms in '50 and '54 when I wasn't even a fantasy in my pops' mind, man. I could stand above all of them, even the ones with their bombs now. I could pay tribute to them with words but still judge them crazy. And it was okay. It felt right to wear two faces, to go back and forth from poetic fury to social condescension or whatever you wanna call it. I thought I had it beat with the education and the poetry and opening up my heart like some long-haired, brown-skinned hippy. And now this. I'm a hypocrite, man."

Like the water from the open fire hydrant, the words had rushed out of him. And yet he couldn't say exactly what it was that troubled him about the attack on his sister, couldn't pinpoint what it was that made his face hot and his blood race angrily in his veins. Willie, silenced by his own impotence, sat looking at him. He knew he could neither urge him on nor discourage him and inevitably he would have to stand aside and let whatever was to happen run its course. His voice almost a whisper, he said, "It's okay, Sixto. I know how it feels. Just let the pain come out, man. Just let it out. Cry if you have to."

But the pain would never leave him. Spics weren't Greeks and the word katharsis had no meaning in private tragedy. Sixto's mind raced back into time, searching for an answer, knowing, even as it fled like a wounded animal seeking refuge from its tormentors, that it was an aimless search. It was like running a maze. Like the rats in the psychology films and the puzzles in the children's section of weekend newspapers. One followed a path with a pencil until he came to a dead end, then retraced his steps. Thousands of years passed before him in a matter of minutes.

The Tainos: a peaceful people, some history books said. No way, he thought. They fought the Spaniards, drowned them to test their immortality. And their *caciques* were as fierce and as brave as Crazy Horse or Geronimo. Proud chiefs they were. Jumacao, Daguao, Yaureibo, Caguax, Agueybaná, Mabodamaca, Aymamón, Urayoán, Orocobix, Guarionex all fought the Spaniards with all they had ... *guasábara* ... *guasábara* ... *guasábara* ... their battle cry echoing through the hills like an eerie phantom; they fought their horses and dogs; they fought their swords and guns and when there was no other recourse, rather than submitting, they climbed sheer cliffs and, holding their children to their breasts, leapt into the sea.

And the blacks: *los negros*, whose blood and heritage he carried. They didn't submit to slavery but escaped and returned to conduct raids against the oppressors, so that the whole *negrito lindo* business, so readily accepted as a term of endearment, was a joke, an appeasement on the part of the Spaniards. The *bombas* and *bembas* and *ginganbó* and their all night dances and *oraciones* to Changó: warrior men of the Jelofe, Mandingo, Mende, Yoruba, Dahomey, Ashanti, Ibo, Fante, Baule and Congo tribes, choosing battle over slavery.

And the Spaniards: certainly not a peaceful people. For centuries they fought each other and then branched out to cross the sea and slaughter hundreds of thousands of Indians, leaving an indelible mark on entire civilizations, raping and pillaging and gutting the earth of its riches, so that when it was all done and they laid in a drunken stupor four hundred years later, their pockets empty, they rose again to fight themselves in civil war.

And way back, way back before El Cid Campeador began to wage war: The Moors. *Los moros* ... *alhambra, alcázar, alcohol, almohada, alcalde, alboroto* ... NOISE ... CRIES OF WAR ... A thousand years the maze traveled and it led to a dead end with dark men atop fleet Arabian stallions, dark men, both in visage and intent, raising their scimitars against those dishonoring their house ... they had invented algebra and Arabic numbers and it all added up to war ... there was no other way ...

"I gotta kill him, bro," Sixto heard himself say. "I gotta. Otherwise I'm as good as dead."

One had to live with himself and that was the worst part of it; he had to live with the knowledge and that particular brand of cowardice that eroded the mind and destroyed one's soul. And it wasn't so much that his sister had been wronged. He'd seen that. The injury came from not retaliating. He was back at the beginning. Banana leaves and coconuts and machete duels at sundown. Just like his father and his *jíbaro* values. For even if the aggressor never talked, even if he never mentioned his act to another soul for whatever reason, there was still another person, another member of the tribe, who could single him out in a crowd and say to himself: "That one belongs to me and so does his sister."

Sixto tried to recall other times when his manhood had been challenged, but it seemed as if everything had happened long ago and hadn't been important. Kid fights over mention of his mother, rights of ownership of an object, a place in the hierarchy of the block, a word said of his person, a lie, a bump by a stranger on a crowded subway train—nothing ever going beyond words or at worst, a sudden shoving match quickly broken up by friends.

But this was different. His brain was not functioning properly, he thought. He tried watching himself, tried to become an observer, the impartial judge of his actions. Through a small opening in his consciousness, he watched the raging battle. His heart called for the blood of the enemy and his brain urged him to use caution. There was no thought of danger, for in that region of struggle, survival meant not so much escaping with his life, but conquering fear and regaining his honor.

Sixto picked up the gun and studied it once more. He pushed the safety to make sure it was locked and placed the gun between the waistband of his pants and the flesh of his stomach. The cold metal sent slivers of ice running down his legs. It was a pleasant sensation, much as if a woman he had desired for some time had suddenly let him know, in an unguarded moment, that intimacy was possible between them. Avoiding Willie's eyes, he walked around the kitchen, pulled out his shirt and let it hang out over his pants. It was important that he learn to walk naturally and reduce his self-consciousness about the weapon. But it was his mind working tricks again. Nobody would notice. The idea was to act calmly. That's what everyone said: the thieves, the cheap stickup men who mugged old people and taxi drivers; the burglars who, like vultures, watched the movement of a family until certain that they were gone, swooped down and cleaned out the apartment, even in the middle of the day; the check specialists, who studied mailboxes as if they were bank vaults so they could break them open and steal welfare checks or fat letters from the island on the chance they might contain money orders or cash. They all said it. Even the young gang kids said it. Don't act suspiciously. Act as if you were going about your business.

Going to shoot someone was like going to work. That was it. He'd carry his books and nobody would suspect that he was carrying death. He laughed inwardly at the immense joke. He'd once seen a film in which Robert Mitchum, posing as a preacher, had pulled a derringer out of a Bible in the final scene. Why not. He'd hollow out his Western Civilization text and place the gun in it. It was his duty. The act was a way of surviving, of earning what was truly his. Whether a pay check or an education, it meant nothing without self-respect.

But the pieces of the puzzle did not fit and Sixto sat down dejectedly. He let his head fall into his hands and for a moment thought he would cry. Willie said still nothing and Sixto waited, listening, the void of silence becoming larger and larger, expanding so that the sounds of the street, a passing car, the excitement of a child, the rushing water from the open hydrant, a mother's window warning retreated, became fainter and seemed to trim the outer edges of the nothingness within the silence. He could hear his own breathing and the beating of his heart and still he waited.

And then slowly, as if waking from a refreshing sleep, Sixto felt himself grow calmer and a pleasant coldness entered his body as heart and mind finally merged and became tuned to his mission. He smiled at the feeling and knew he had gone through the barrier of doubt and fear which had been erected to protect him from himself, to make sure he did not panic at the last moment. War had to be similar. He had heard the older young men, the ones who had survived Vietnam, talk about it. Sonny Maldonado with his plastic foot, limping everywhere he went, quiet and unassuming, talked about going through a doorway and into a quiet room where one died a little and then came out again, one's mind alive but the rest of the body already dead to the upcoming pain.

It had finally happened, he thought. There was no anger or regret, no rationalizations concerning future actions. No more justifications or talk about honor and dignity. Instead, Sixto perceived the single objective coldly. There was neither danger nor urgency in carrying out the sentence and avenging the wrong. It seemed almost too simple. If it took years he knew the task would be accomplished. He would study the habits of his quarry, chart his every movement, and one day he'd strike. He would wait in a deserted hallway some late night, calmly walk out of the shadows, only his right index finger and his brain connected and say: "How you doing, Lino?" and his voice alone would convey the terrible message. Sixto smiled to himself and saw, as in a slow motion cinematic shot, his mind's ghost delicately squeeze the trigger repeatedly, the small animal muzzle of the gun following Lino Quintana's body as it fell slowly and hit the floor, the muscles of his victim's face twitching and life ebbing away forever. It happened all the time and no one was ever discovered.

Sixto laughed, almost too loudly. He took the gun out from under his shirt and placed it resolutely on the table. "I gotta think some more, man," he said. "That's crazy rushing into the thing. You wanna a beer, Willie?"

Willie was not convinced of his friend's newly found calm. Reluctantly, he accepted the beer. He watched Sixto and tried to measure the depth of his eyes. They had become strangely flat, the glint of trust in them absent. It was as if a thin, opaque veil had been sewn over the eyes to mask Sixto's emotions. He felt helpless but said nothing. He opened the beer and began mourning the loss. Sixto was right, he thought. It was Spanish roulette. Spics were born and the cylinder spun. When it stopped one was handed the gun and, without looking, had to bring it to one's head, squeeze the trigger and take his chances.

The belief was pumped into the bloodstream, carved into the flesh through generations of strife, so that being was the enactment of a ritual rather than the beginning of a new life. One never knew his own reactions until faced with Sixto's dilemma. And yet the loss would be too great, the upcoming grief too profound and the ensuing suffering eternal. The violence would be passed on to another generation to be displayed as an invisible coat of arms, much as Sixto's answer had come to him as a relic. His friend would never again look at the world with wonder, and poetry would cease to spring from his heart. If he did write, the words would be guarded, careful, full of excuses and apologies for living. Willie started to raise the beer in a toast but thought better of it and set the can on the table.

"Whatever you do, bro," he said, "be careful."

"Don't worry, man," Sixto replied. "I got the thing under control." He laughed once again and suddenly his eyes were ablaze with hatred. He picked up the gun, stuck it back into his pants and stood up. "No good, man," he said, seemingly to himself, and rushed out, slamming the door of the apartment behind him.

Beyond the sound of the door, Willie could hear the whirring cylinder as it began to slow down, each minute click measuring the time before his friend had to raise the weapon to his head and kill part of himself.

CASUALTY REPORT

As he had for the past four days, Sonny Maldonado spent the afternoon waiting. With one part of his mind, which he felt couldn't be trusted, he imagined something had failed and the police had finally caught up with them. Shortly after two o'clock the phone rang. Expecting to hear Romero's voice, he moved tensely to pick up the receiver. Disappointedly, he listened to his sister reminding him again of the hospital's visiting hours. She was on the verge of tears. After spending time calming her down, he agreed to see his father that evening. He said goodbye and hated himself for lying, knowing he could do nothing until it was over. He sensed that once this latest plan was in motion, the matter would never be finished. Like a bad habit, the destruction would continue, each action plunging them deeper into the hell.

He still woke up at night, the nausea choking him as he fought off the smell of death, repeating to himself that he was home and safe until the nightmare was over. He thought then, after his sister's call, that they'd tried phoning him during that time. Going to the front of the apartment, he raised the blind and, shielding his eyes from the spring sunlight, turned his attention to the street. He felt a few seconds of apprehension as he imagined them coming in person. The idea was against security measures and he quickly discarded the notion.

Relaxed for the moment, he watched the movement below. Nothing much changed from one day to the next. As if played upon a stage, people's actions had become repetitive and without meaning. Moving back and forth on the slate-like surface of the street, they appeared strangely lifeless. They were like wooden figures whose invisible strings were being manipulated by a power much too great to combat: semi-discreet drug sales; men playing dominoes in front of the *bodega*; a police car cruising slowly down the block to send truants scurrying for cover into stinking hallways; young prostitutes, their faces sickly grayish, their hair still in rollers, making ready for another evening out; each scene painted in the most minute detail, but somehow devoid of humanity.

From his perch five stories above, he followed a fat, seal-like woman in a ragged coat. She was a white woman with no apparent connection to anyone on the block. As in a trance she was often seen walking her two equally fat dogs, never speaking or looking at anyone, always clutching her ragged coat in winter or summer, her mouth moving silently as she repeated some obscure litany of sorrow, her white face clashing glaringly against the darker ones of the neighborhood. The woman took one long mournful look up the street and entered the building. He imagined a young addict waiting inside the building to take whatever money remained in her pocketbook. Here, a day didn't pass without someone being attacked or having his apartment broken into.

Half expecting a figure to rush out of the building with the woman's pocketbook, Maldonado lowered the blind and turned away from the window. He wanted no part of it. Involvement, even at that distance, would only serve to fill him with remorse about his own impotence. There was no truth in what Romero had said. One single act did not change the course of history. For no matter how much he turned it over in his mind, in each act there were always two victims. Lately, it had become impossible for him to determine which had suffered the greater injury, the attacker or his prey. He shook his head violently as the sharp pain of the question stabbed at his brain. He didn't want to think about difficult things.

Walking across the neat, but sparsely furnished living room, he paused in front of the television set. He was again struck by the absence of the photograph above the large mahogany cabinet of the TV. How long had it sat there evoking past glories before he understood what he had endured those four years. Like a membrane being lifted surgically from his mind's eye, he'd slowly grown to question his obedience to the code which he'd once accepted as salvation from his past. During the last year he came to despise himself in the high-necked tunic and stiff hat. Finally, enraged by the shattering of his illusions, he'd hurled the picture against the wall. He didn't view the act as a closing statement on a chapter of his life, but more as an act of defiance against a hallowed concept.

After turning on the set he sat down. Cartoon figures materialized on the gray screen, a self-conscious smile creased Maldonado's thin face. The animals screeched, whirled, ran, made odd noises and bounced violently into walls, returning each time to start once more their senseless attempts at destroying themselves and each other. He enjoyed the simplicity of the struggle, but wondered what went on in the minds of their creators. His face grew momentarily hot as he imagined having to explain, in some future criticism-self-criticism session, that he'd spent the afternoon watching cartoons instead of reading from the selections assigned for study. Romero had explained that most entertainment was a diversion from the group's ultimate purpose and that all entertainment was designed to keep people's minds hazy. He didn't agree totally with their analysis, but he hadn't said anything. As usual, the words remained locked within him. Rising suddenly, he switched channels, found nothing which would meet with the group's approval and finally turned off the set.

Walking to the bookshelf, which his wife had set up, he extracted a small red book. He studied the thin Asiatic face on the cover, the sparse beard, the pained eyes, and attempted to read the writing of his one-time enemy. He read the title, *Some Considerations on the Colonial Question*, several times. It was no use. Beyond his chronic difficulty with reading, the words were doubly foreign to him. They seemed to tell nothing about hunger and cold, about distance between people who, by every right, should be brothers. There was no mention of loneliness, of Christmases filled with sadness as he lay awake hoping for a small gift, a windup car, a picture book, anything to stave off going downstairs to face his friends empty-handed. He wanted to believe the words, but they didn't explain walking through the gray slush of winter in torn shoes; they didn't explain his sitting in school wanting to learn and not being able to because everything was in English and too fast for him, the daily ordeal making him ashamed and anxious to return home to make sure his mother and sister were safe. The words, neat, even, standing boldly against the white paper of the small book, told nothing of the rage of wanting and not knowing what it was he wanted, of feeling a stranger no matter where he stood. They explained nothing about looking at himself in the mirror and not recognizing the image because it was dark and as foreign as the enemy's had been. Sonny Maldonado closed the book and looked again at the old man's face. He was a hero to his people, but he didn't look like a hero. All those years of waiting and fighting, of running and hiding and having faith and courage like Romero had said. How had it happened? How did a person survive all that? Where did the courage and conviction come from? He still wondered how he himself had managed to stay alive. Kill or be killed. That was the motto. Not *Semper Fidelis*.

He was sick the first time. For days he couldn't bring himself to believe that the neat hole below the right eye had been able to paralyze his victim and render him lifeless. Nor could he initially believe that it was his doing until one of the others turned the body over with his foot and he saw the hollow skull and the spilt grayish red mass. The dreaded enemy he'd been taught to search and destroy was only a boy, perhaps fourteen, with features soft and delicate like those of the teenage prostitutes in Saigon. "It's like bowling," Traynor'd said, patting him on the back, his cowboy words trying to make things easier for him. "You'll get used to it. Just think of them as pins."

But he hadn't gotten used to it. The boy's face haunted him afterwards and he never felt sure-handed again when raising his rifle to a firing position, the expert medal he'd worn so proudly on his leaves home slowly becoming a symbol of shame. Occasionally, when he least expected it, the boy still appeared in his dreams walking a water buffalo, he and the boy, smiling, walking in a grassy field or fishing side by side, the scene shifting from a canal back then to another time further back in his memory. The two of them at the lake in Central Park where they'd caught goldfish and were carrying them home in a milk container. He and the barefoot boy with the little hole below his eye walking down Lexington Avenue, joking and stopping to look into store windows or to buy an ice. Sometimes, in his dreams, he saw himself lying on the grass, the bloody grayish mass serving as a pillow for his head, the black dime-sized hole alive with insects, so that he woke up clawing his face, and Carmen cried and held him like he was a child having a bad dream populated by harmless monsters.

So long ago and he still wished he hadn't fired. He still imagined yelling to warn the boy. Perhaps if he'd made an attempt at a warning, the death wouldn't still bother him. The thought that warning the boy might've resulted in his own death, as it had been suggested by Traynor and Mancuso and the captain, offered him no consolation. There had been others after the boy, but there was no choice and there was never again the chance to stop and inspect the damage, telling himself later that he wasn't sure any of his bullets had found a target. Towards the end he always made sure he fired high or into the ground, living in constant fear that the others, whose lives depended on him, would consider him a traitor.

When he came home he'd almost fought with his cousin, not understanding how Carlos could brag about how he'd killed the Vietnamese, whom he still called "slopes." Carlos apologized but things were never the same between them. Carlos told his sister that he didn't understand what had gotten into him. "Sonny was never like that," he said, and bragged again that a gook was a gook and he'd killed enough of them to know.

Maldonado rubbed his bad leg, pushed down on the plastic appendage which the doctors had affixed to his ankle—and which no amount of kindness, on anyone's part, could bring him to call his foot—and stood up. He was still intrigued by the last meeting with Romero, Pacheco and Mora. They had been sincere, he thought, in praising him for his part in the last "action," as they called it. What had he done? At exactly two o'clock in the morning he'd stopped his floor buffing machine, told Richards he had to make a phone call, and went down the hall to a phone booth. He'd dialed the radio station and read the communiqué. The next day the papers reported it as "a man with a noticeably Spanish accent." A week later when he met with the group, Romero asked him if he had hired someone to read the message. He'd begun explaining but Romero said he was kidding. It was the first time he'd seen Romero laugh.

But it was to be different now and he had protested their trust in him, going as far as questioning their wisdom in choosing someone with a noticeable handicap to carry out the plan. They had lowered their heads understandingly and Romero had spoken their own revered leader's name, whose picture was displayed prominently at the meeting place and whose eyes had the same determination as Ho Chi Minh: *La patria es valor y sacrificio*, the homeland is courage and sacrifice. His grandmother had once met Don Pedro when she was a young girl in Cacimar. She was a *nacionalista* and speaking in reverential terms, referred to him as *el maestro*. She had also known Lolita Lebrón, but, like so many others, bad times had made her quit. He wondered if his grandmother would've been involved in the attack on the U.S. Congress. It angered him that they'd think he was protesting because he lacked courage. He held his temper in check, controlling the violent urge to tell them that they were the ones who were afraid to go themselves. Instead, he told them that if they felt he was the right person for the job this time, he'd do it. Romero nodded and used him to illustrate how a true revolutionary put his own feelings aside and understood the true purpose of his mission. They all agreed and criticized themselves for the times they had allowed their quest for personal glory to stand in the way of the task. He wished he could speak like them, but he'd never been much of a talker. In any case, he couldn't follow everything they discussed. He felt doubly ashamed when they explained that they'd chosen him because the intended target was only a few blocks from where he worked and he knew the neighborhood. So it was done. In less than twenty-four hours he'd be back at war.

Maldonado stood by the bookshelf, looked once more at Ho's face on the book cover, placed the slim volume back in its slot, and returned to his post at the window. Children had taken over the street. Their laughter and curses crackled in the afternoon sunshine, the voices far away as if his own childhood were beckoning to him. A stickball game was in progress. He tried to keep track of the game, but his mind was consumed with his part of the plan. Something had to have happened or they would've called by now.

Angrily, he walked back to the bookshelf and turned on the radio to the all news station. A double murder in Brooklyn, news of Kissinger's latest visit abroad, a four alarm fire in the Bronx, the stock market report, weather, sports. Nothing was mentioned which gave him any clue that anything had gone wrong. It had been four months since the last time. The next day, stations carried the story the entire day, describing in detail the aftermath of the blast.

He turned off the radio and sat down dejectedly. There was nothing to do but wait. That was always the worst part. Your mind took over and made you think about all the things that could go wrong. He didn't want to think about all the waiting he'd done in the Corps. Hurry up and wait. In every case, however, you had to wait and tell yourself not to worry, to be patient.

He tried pushing the thought away but recalled waiting crouched in the tall grass, his breath coming in silent little gasps, watching the small figure approach and then kneeling, raising the rifle, aiming and before he knew it, squeezing the trigger and watching the boy's rifle fly in the air and the boy disappear from sight so that at first he thought he'd missed. That first time the wait hadn't been too long, but he recalled other times when he waited flat on his stomach, the damp undergrowth making his body cold while his face ran with sweat, the sounds of the jungle, the birds and insects going about their business, their noises and calls coming to him clearly, while far away like some demonic soundtrack the insistent drumming of automatic fire was punctuated by the thud and whining of mortars. The two forces, one driven by nature and life, the other by man's hatred and death, keeping his mind split. Why did his mind produce all these thoughts? Where did they come from?

He waited then, listening, the strange sing-song voices coming closer, the feeling of doom growing bigger and his insides shrinking with fear. His mouth dry and his throat thick, the fear becoming like a needle thrust deep into his groin.

They had come so close he could smell their sweat and see the stitching where they had repaired their clothing.

Even when you had given up all hope of surviving and had crossed into that other world where nothing mattered except not feeling the fear, you had to wait. Tony Sánchez, his stomach torn open, had to wait for the chopper to lift him out. The medics had fixed him up until they got him to the hospital. Once there they stopped the bleeding and ran a bottle into his arm. He had to wait until the doctors got through with guys who had half their body shot off, or had lost a leg or an arm, yet still could be salvaged. Sánchez had been so badly wounded, his insides so mangled, Traynor'd said, that triage had given up and listed him as "Killed in Action" in the casualty report. He'd never seen a casualty report but Traynor said it was made up every day. How many killed, how many wounded, how many missing in action. And then, after all the waiting they operated on Tony for eight hours and he pulled through only to come home and get knifed in the heart in an argument in the Bronx. Spics were born to wait. He banged the window frame with his fist, his jaw clenched tight against the memories.

Down below, Santiago, his fat stomach sticking out, was watching the high school girls coming home. As he peeked out through the plate glass window of the barber shop, he looked like an animal waiting to spring forward and snare his prey. Santiago had the glass painted with a scene of the island. Green palms and blue water. Off to the side there was a brown "hooch": a *bohío*, Carmen had called it. It was the Indian word for house. Carmen had told him all the books said the Tainos were wiped out by the Spaniards, but that couldn't be true because he looked like an Indian. Cochise. That's what Traynor called him. Tommy Garza was Mexican and really looked like an Indian. Traynor called him Geronimo. It was a big joke and he hadn't minded until they got Tommy. His buddy, Valenzuela, went crazy and said he was going to frag Traynor if he kept it up. Tommy Garza was color blind, so they used him to spot the enemy in the jungle. All he saw was the dark shapes, outlines, never the colors. Maldonado imagined not being able to see color. It didn't make sense, just gray shapes as Tommy had explained. Tommy had tripped over a mine. The explosion ripped up into him and left only his torso, right about where the ribs began. Gray shapes. It didn't make sense.

Nothing made sense. Not what happened then, nor what was about to happen now. Even though Romero hadn't mentioned it, he knew it was no longer a question of leaving incendiary devices in department stores or blowing out bank windows at four in the morning. There was a special feeling to it this time. He could sense it.

Just as he'd sensed Captain Hemming's mood before they went into the village and were ordered to burn it in spite of the women and children still in the flimsy shacks. He knew innocent people would be injured again this time. It didn't make sense and he wished there was some way he could ask out.

Maldonado spent the rest of the afternoon wrestling with his conscience, trying to identify the enemy clearly. Towards evening, after his wife, Carmen, came home from work and began cooking, he lay down to arrange his thoughts. He'd gone through the nervousness of waiting and crossed into a sullen mood of resignation in which he felt helpless to control the outcome of the situation and therefore was no longer involved in its emotion. It was better this way, he thought. He wanted a clear head when the call came. He knew now it would come. For a moment he was curious about the caller's identity, but quickly drove the thought away. He knew it was best that the caller remain faceless, as he'd remain to the caller. The other phases of the operation: assembling the device, bringing it to the pickup place, typing the message for the media, contacting the police after the action, all these would come from other groups. He knew they existed, but had never met their members. If he had met them it had been accidentally and without any knowledge of their involvement. Romero had explained the practicality of such a method and he'd understood. It was the best way to avoid infiltration. If someone in a group was caught and forced to give up information, the other groups would be safe. He wondered if he'd break under questioning. Perhaps if he were tortured he might. He steered his mind away from the subject. It did no good to dwell on things which couldn't be tested until they happened.

Through the open window of the bedroom at the end of the four-room railroad apartment, he watched the approaching darkness, the shadows falling rapidly over the tenements, stilling for another day their reality and allowing every one to begin his nightly illusion of a better day to come. He loved day's end and a wistful feeling of peacefulness came over him. He lay quietly now, concentrating, listening to the sounds drifting across the empty lot below the window.

The lot was like a barometer of the despair. Bricks, bottles, garbage, discarded refrigerators and stoves, and a car engine littered the open spaces between the two buildings. Each day something new was added. One time it'd been a brown and yellow hobby horse. The toy had landed upright in one of the scant patches of brush growing in the black earth. The plastic animal looked strangely real. He'd brought down his field glasses and looked through them. The field glasses were a souvenir, cut away from the legless body of a North Vietnamese regular after a skirmish. The glasses were huge Russian-made binoculars. Whenever he thought of them he told himself he'd never be a communist, although he wasn't clear what it meant. Through the powerful lenses he saw the two handles on the sides of the horse's neck. He'd thought the animal was a dog and the truth had angered him.

The constant accumulation of garbage had concerned him when he and Carmen moved into the apartment three years before. Back then he recalled the small, neat, American towns he'd visited on his way west. They were sedate, pleasant towns near which he'd been stationed. Like photographs in an album, the images remained with him, kept and treasured as contrast against what he'd known growing up. Rather than the squalor and chaos of his childhood, his memories were replaced by even rows of brightly painted houses, carefully kept lawns, clipped hedges and tall, stately trees with branches raised to cloudless skies.

He'd felt good about these people whom he, after so many years of torment, finally joined in a common objective. Walking down their streets in his uniform, he'd felt part of them. He was their protector and they seemed happy that he was among them. There never seemed to be any garbage in those towns. Empty lots, yes, but no garbage in them. Not even a broken bottle. He'd wondered at the people's neatness, their calm, the control which they exercised over each aspect of their lives and how they managed to hide all traces of everyday living. But the girl had opened his eyes. Without meaning to, she'd made him see it all.

He met her while waiting for the bus back to the base. She'd offered him a ride and he'd shrugged his shoulders and accepted shyly. Once he was in the car, she had introduced herself and was then full of questions about him, talking to him as if they had known each other for years. When she found out he was Puerto Rican, she went into an explanation of a book she had recently read about a Puerto Rican who had been a convict and an addict. She said the book was called *Down These Mean Streets*. Maldonado told her he'd never heard of it, wishing she'd stop talking about books. After he'd met Carmen she had read parts of it to him and he liked it. But back then he hadn't heard of the book and he was embarrassed, as he had always been whenever someone mentioned reading. Chattering away, the girl told him all about the book and asked him if things had been like that when he was growing up. "We had to read the book for a sociology class." He shrugged his shoulders. She kept on talking, asking him if he'd ever met anyone like the characters in the book, making him dredge up memories and making him wish she'd stop the car so he could get out.

But he liked her, liked the sound of her voice, the English words so crisp and clear. "Do you know where the neighborhood is? The writer makes it sound like there's a lot of people using heroin in that neighborhood," she said. "That's impossible. It's fiction. He's making it up." Feeling ashamed, he agreed. "Yeah, it's just a couple of people," he'd said, the lie making his face hot because so many of his friends ended up shooting heroin. They saw each other again: the movies, a coke and hamburger, a walk; harmless hand-holding and, when saying goodnight, swift, fleeting kisses which made his head spin and left her fragrance with him. One evening she opened the door to the car and when he got in he didn't say anything until they were on the highway, traveling away from the town. She then asked him what was going to happen to him if he went to Vietnam. As he always did, he shrugged his shoulders. She mentioned going to Canada. "A lot of boys are doing it," she said. He didn't understand her and she didn't press the issue, but he felt as if they had grown closer during those brief moments, as if she cared what happened to him. He also realized that she thought the war was wrong. This puzzled him, but he didn't want to think about the subject.

He allowed the girl, Ann, to drive him away from the town until she parked the car on a secluded dirt road. They got out and walked to the top of a hill. In the dusk he saw the dump below. There were rats scurrying over the mounds of debris. The sight angered him. All at once he understood how it was accomplished, the neatness and the order. Rather than accepting the knowledge, he felt a deep, consuming rage. It was as if his mind had snapped and the anger was flowing in his veins, making him dizzy. Why had she brought him up there? Did she know he was lying about his neighborhood? He felt completely without defenses and as if she had brought him there to show him where he belonged, where he had come from.

Up to that point Ann had been a fair goddess to be respected, about whom he had woven intricate fantasies of tenderness. She suddenly became soiled. Her bright smile became a smirk, her lips tawdry and her body a vessel into which he could now empty his disgust. When they returned to the car he kissed her roughly and then reached his hand first into her blouse, to almost brutally fondle her breasts, and then between her legs. She did not protest and the word *puta* repeated itself over and over in his mind. Without a word, he worked her skirt up while she arched herself to help him remove her underpants. The revulsion he felt at her willingness and his sudden hatred was so total that a powerful wave of nausea almost made him stop. His other encounters with sex had been with easy Puerto Rican girls, ones who gave it away to anyone for a nice word, a good rap, stupid lovesick high school dropouts working at the five and ten and dying to get out of their parents' houses. In Ann—he did not recall her last name afterward—he thought he had found an ideal, a perfection, a respite from all he had known up to meeting her.

His genuine attraction to her added to the feeling of confusion, of passionate need and the overpowering self-hatred brewing inside of him. Once inside of her, his mind ablaze with images of destruction, in which his penis would reach into her entrails, and like the images he'd had of meeting the enemy in hand to hand combat, her guts, the bluish entrails Sergeant McIver had talked about, would come spilling out of her lower stomach. He had wanted to kill her. The noises she made in her passionate abandon added to his fury. When he finally released his anger in a final thrust, her body stiffened and she cried out and then lay limply, her head as if it had broken off from her neck as it rested against the car door. He zipped himself up and sat staring at the night.

A few minutes later she opened her gray eyes and smiled at him. He hadn't been able to respond. Instead he wanted to slap her face and watch the fair skin grow red from his fingertips. He'd ordered her to drive to the top of the hill. He remained immobile for a long time, looking at the town lights, everything far away and as if in a dream. Sensing something had gone wrong, the girl remained still. As he sat, shocks of anger flooded his mind again and again. Finally, he took the back of her neck, and fighting the revulsion of her thick flaxen hair, pushed her face against his lap. Without the least resistance, even unzipping his pants, she obliged him, swallowing his seed which he had allowed himself to believe up to that night would someday be their offspring. Everything happened very quickly. Afterward he sat back and, alone with himself, felt the darkness of the dump envelope him in sorrow. He stared again at the lights of the town and then at the sky and it seemed as if one were a reflection of the other, as if the world had turned upside down. He felt remorseful then and held himself to her, more as an expression of his grief than from any need she may have had for warmth.

Later, near the front gate of the base, he apologized, but the girl shook her head slowly, still smiling her even-toothed smile, her eyes dumb and still giving. She said he shouldn't, that everything would be all right. She said her parents were going out of town the following weekend and would he spend the time with her, since she was going back to college the week after.

He nodded and then said goodnight. The next day he went to Sergeant McIver and explained that he had a girl and needed some time with her. McIver laughed. "So you found yourself a Mexican *chiquita*. No problem, *amigo*. McIver'll get you a three-day pass quicker than you can say *enchilada*." He wanted to tell McIver that the girl wasn't Mexican, to show him the picture in his wallet, but he didn't.

The following week Ann picked him up and they drove to the coast. Completely relaxed, they laughed and swam and ate seafood. He'd told her things about himself he'd never revealed to anyone: the small disappointments of his life, the far away dreams all came spilling out of him easily. She listened and encouraged him, soothing him when things became difficult. But alone that night in her parents' house, when by all rights their love making should've been intense, he found that he was unable to enjoy himself. His mind wandered and he became preoccupied with thoughts of someone breaking in on them. Not until a year later when he woke up from the amputation did he realize how hurt he'd been by his realization near the town dump. He had grasped in an almost primitive way, that his anger had not come from seeing the dump, but from the destruction of his innocence about America, which had always been held up to him as perfection, a vision to strive for, a reality totally different from his squalor.

When he moved into the apartment with Carmen the empty lot with its garbage was a reminder of those days, when eager to escape he had taken the easiest way out of the misery he was certain his life would become. The lot was a reminder of a life he thought he'd left behind. The lot branded him. And yet after only a few months with Carmen, he became used once more to the cluttered lot and the accompanying noise of the surrounding tenements, the monotonous pace of the neighborhood. He now accepted the garbage-filled lot, much as he had grown to accept the other backyards of his childhood; he had given up on the idea of a house with a backyard sandbox and swings for the children to come; he had rationalized the disorder of the neighborhood and the stench which rose from the empty lot in the summer as part of living in the city. It was their town dump and they had as much right to it as the Americans had to theirs. It was the only way to keep an apartment clean. Except that he and Carmen kept their own clean and fresh in the worst weather without resorting to throwing garbage out the window. There was something deeper about people dumping garbage out of their windows but he hadn't been able to figure it out.

Lying on the wide double bed, the flowered spread like an Indian carpet beneath his body, he lapsed into a half-waking state and gave himself up to nightfall. Sounds and smells of evening came to him in pleasurable waves: the steady rhythm of pounded mortars as garlic was mashed, the hissing of meat as it hit melted lard. They were sounds and smells which quelled hunger at its most basic level, that of anticipation. It was one of the few memories of childhood which he recalled with fondness. Behind the waves of cooking food he now heard bits of conversation. English and Spanish. Rising and falling like notes on a musical scale. Around the voices and the smells, like an aura, TV and radio sounds: *merengues, mambos, guaguancós, salsa*, rhythm and blues, rock, "I Dream of Jeannie", "Gilligan's Island", "Star Trek", RADIO WADO ... W-A-D-O Radioooo ... all of it blending like a crazy unrehearsed orchestra, dissonant and yet melodious in its familiarity.

Above the din, a woman was pleading with her children to finish their home-work and clear the kitchen table before their father got home. Her voice was desperate; in it, a combination of fear and delight. She spoke first in English and then in Spanish, punctuating the last sentence with an explosive *¡CARAJO!* He liked the sounds of words and smiled at the curse word. Words changed in color and texture and at times said things all by themselves. Sometimes a swear word had more love in it than a kind word.

He thought now about night. When he couldn't sleep he lay awake going over the incidents of his life which he had never understood. The voices outside his window would sometimes become angry and loud, their tones harsh and stripped of any human quality, as people battered each other mercilessly, alternating as they stated each grievance, issuing threats, their hearts bleeding but neither side admitting the pain, the words disguised with false courage. Man and woman, lovers, children and parents, all of them intent on winning. At those times the words seemed to hang in a void. In other apartments conversations ceased, all music was muted and everyone listened in on the quarrel.

Sometimes the fights went on all night and into early morning. Once in a while the police were called in to calm things, this quite seldom, since they invariably went away empty-handed. To those involved in the dispute the interruption was a relief, an opportunity to show the other party that their love was still intact as they united against a common enemy, defending passionately the antagonist, stating with great conviction that their disagreements were not a matter for the police, the controversy being nothing more than a misunderstanding. Whether because of fear of reprisals, lost love, or merely the fact that insults, beatings, ridicule, both public and private, and the rest that went with the endless arguments were better than loneliness, the people hung on to each other with a desperation, which he understood and accepted.

Although the maze of emotions through which each of these people had to travel in order to reach another was complicated and made him feel like a stranger, he accepted his tie to them, knowing the link was permanent and would be with him forever. He thought this as night closed in and he felt a twinge of contempt for his life. The feeling lasted only a moment and then he was back inside himself. He had grown calmer since losing his foot. It was as if in having rid himself of a part of his body so vital to locomotion, he had accepted the pointlessness of escape from his life. The same applied to these people, except that they had not yet accepted their fate; they still fought desperately for some measure of dignity with each other, if not the rest of the world. What Romero had pointed out to him was true. All the aberrations of character in the people were a sign of their lack of dignity: the dope addicts, the dealers, the drunks, the prostitutes, the thieves, wife-beaters, drunks, child molesters, street gamblers, gang members, phony welfare recipients and the ones who stood by and tolerated their behavior. Although victims of an inhuman system which denied them dignity, they were all thumbing their noses at any pretense of equality.

For as long as Puerto Rico was a colony, not one person could hold his head high. Deep within their beings, in spite of their behavior, each knew that he must walk with eyes downcast because the land of his birth or the land of his parents' birth was not a free place. That's why he had joined them. In accepting to go and place the device, he hoped someone would listen.

He again wished the call would come. The last time it had come quickly. The following day he had gone to the address, dialed the police number and read the statement, difficult as reading had been. Now it was four days and no call. For him there would be no dialing this time, no reading of messages, no letters to tape under a phone booth stand. All he had to do was pick up the device when he got off work in the morning, walk with it to the tavern, go in as if he wanted to use the bathroom and place the device in the garbage. They said George Washington had come there to eat. Maldonado couldn't tell if they were joking. The device would go off during the lunch hour when the place was packed with Wall Street executives. There were sure to be casualties. He hoped there were no children involved. It was now five days since he'd gotten the assignment. Maybe he should call Romero. He decided not to, since it would disturb Romero's wife. She was expecting their first child. Did she know? Romero always stressed how important it was to keep family out of it. But Carmen knew, and as he lay staring at the darkened sky, he again worried that he'd made the wrong decision in telling her.

His internal debate concerning Carmen developed no further. It was better that she know. "If I know, then I don't have to worry that it's another woman," she'd said. She was always kind. He had laughed, wanting to tell her that she had nothing to worry about on that account, since nobody would want a cripple. But he hadn't said anything, aware that she'd be hurt if he spoke that way. There had been no one else since he'd met Carmen four years ago. Thinking about it made him want her near. He saw himself touching her face and going over her almost child-like body as if it were the first time.

Recalling the certainty with which Carmen had asserted her claim to him made him feel stronger. For the first time that day he felt a surge of power in his body. Like a small engine turning over, he felt the energy in the middle of his chest. It was as if his veins were being pumped with new blood, his arms and legs, his fingertips charged, and as if an electrical current were passing through him.

But he had to wait now. Nothing must interfere with the process until it was all over. He needed a clear mind, and being with Carmen left him dazed, sleepy and a little frightened and in awe of what she could do for him. For hours afterwards all he saw was her beautiful brown face wherever he went: the large dark eyes so brave and loving and yet so innocent that it made his heart expand each time he looked at her, smiling tenderly at him whenever he looked troubled, telling him, without speaking the words, that everything was all right and he was correct in whatever he chose to do—and without the least amount of reserve, openly, tears coming into her eyes, telling him how much he meant to her and that she loved him. It was best to remain away from her now. It was best and she knew it. She was a smart girl, much smarter than he was. All his energies had to be directed towards the objective and for a moment his mind crossed the line from memory into remembered dreams.

The screams had come to him in his sleep. He jumped up, awake instantly. Very far away he heard the bombers on a run to the north and then silence. He listened intently, as he'd been taught. Perhaps they were under attack and all hell would break loose in the next minute. He groped for the sidearm which he kept near him. The screams came again, this time louder, more pained, confirming that they hadn't been part of a dream. He crawled out of his bunk and shook Traynor awake.

"What is it, buddy?" Traynor said.

"Did you hear it?"

"I heard it."

"What the hell's going on, man?"

"They're interrogating a slope, buddy. Go back to sleep. Emory said they caught him snooping around this afternoon. Claims he was looking for his little sister. Don't worry about it."

He'd gone back to sleep, but the screams woke him up again and he remained awake the rest of the night, listening, fascinated by the agony, wanting to find out what was causing this other man so much pain. Towards sunrise there was one long scream and then silence again. The silence lasted no more than an hour before the din of automatic fire and mortars began another day. He didn't ask anyone about the screams until four days later when, during a lull in a skirmish, he wished to know again what'd happened that night. Traynor didn't want to talk about it, but Vance Russell, the Indian, said they'd hooked up wires to the man.

"It's the only way they can get the slopes to talk," Russell said.

"Get outta here," he'd said, disbelieving.

"Yeah, they're like Indians," Russell went on. "They take a lot of pain, so they wire them up to a generator."

"Electric wires?" he asked, stupidly.

"Yeah, you dumb Puerto Rican," Black Thompson had said, laughing. "They sit him in a chair buck naked, tie him up real good with his legs spread and then wire up the dude's Johnson. Army does that kind of shit. Corps'd just shoot the mothafucka. What's his name, the little eyetalian in B, Monte, said there's a real sicko colonel over there that was a POW in Korea. The dude even plays with the dude's Johnson, gets him real hard before they shoot the juice into him the first time. That's some sick shit, man."

He'd wanted to find out more, but they were being fired on again and Lieutenant Joyce wanted everyone quiet so he could hear the radio. All through the day he tried to imagine the scene, but it kept fading. For the next three weeks things became so hectic that he didn't have time to think about it. Toro, Elias Cruz from 100th Street, Bobby Melendez, Tato Cabrera, Joey Torres, Nino Marchand and Chino, the medic. One after the other, as if the other side had singled out Puerto Ricans and were intent on picking them off one by one. That's when he first found out about the casualty report.

He remembered it all and now he lay very still, listening to his breathing, hoping that nothing had gone wrong. He opened his eyes and stared at the picture of the Sacred Heart, framed and hanging above the dresser. The picture shone faintly in the darkened room and he wished he believed in God again and could pray. Hail Mary, full of grace ... Carmen still believed in God, but it had never caused any problems between them. He was proud of that. Nothing much bothered her. *Ave María, Madre de Dios, bendita seas entre todas las mujeres y bendito sea el fruto de tu vientre, Jesús.* He liked the sing-song of the Rosary and the solemn faces of the women, their dark veils and withered hands, the dark cool quiet of the church, the words drifting from their mouths to hang like angels above him. He had visited the church in Cacimar once and knelt with his grandmother while she prayed. He had been eight and his mother sent him down to the island until his father found work. They remained in the church a long time and he'd felt better, safer for a long time.

But it was all wrong. All of it. He didn't understand it, but it wasn't right. God should provide for all or for none. That much he knew. Religion didn't make sense. He remembered the Buddhist monk in Saigon setting himself on fire. Everyone had laughed, but he'd been horrified and couldn't stop asking himself why. Lieutenant Joyce had come over and asked him if he was all right. He'd shrugged his shoulders and asked why the monk had killed himself. "That's what they believe," Joyce had said. "By extinguishing life, they extinguish the source of suffering, desires." In every religion they wanted you to give up something.

It was crazy. It didn't matter anyhow. He had sinned against God's Law and had been punished. He didn't know where the notion had come from, but he had broken God's Law by killing the boy and couldn't forgive himself. The boy's face appeared before him now. He was speaking Vietnamese, pleading, but Sonny couldn't understand him. He shook his head violently and the image went away.

The sun had settled behind the buildings on the other side of Manhattan so that the room was in total darkness. There was now a soft velvety smoothness to the air drifting in through the open window. Above the sounds of the neighborhood, a voice sang to itself. It was a young girl, perhaps fourteen. The voice was high and although not beautiful, quite strong. There was no fear or self-consciousness in the girl. It was an old song *Fichas Negras*, a bolero. His father would sing it sometimes, the words mournful and filled with a sense of loss as it explains how a man lost a woman he loved like a gambler loses in a game of chance, black chips ... *Yo te perdí, como pierde un buen jugador* ... It was all he could remember of the song.

Of his father he recalled even less, other than the fact that he was gone all day, gone before he got up for school, returning home after he'd gone to bed, never saying anything to anyone on weekends, mostly sitting as in a stupor. There was one year when they went to Central Park to watch baseball games and his father had explained patiently what each player was doing and why. It was the only time he ever saw his father smile. He had tried playing baseball to please his father, but he hadn't been very good at it and eventually gave up the game.

The girl sang on, her voice rich with desire and love, singing as if she knew instinctively the full meaning of the words, somehow preparing herself for the eventual letdown of losing in love. He wished his father were not dying, not here anyway. He'd wanted to return to the island, but stayed on each year, being brave and dreaming.

"Sonny?"

The voice was a shade above a whisper. When he turned, Carmen's hand was on his face. She sat on the edge of the bed and in the darkness he saw her smiling, nodding at him as she always did.

"How you doing?" he said, self-consciously.

"I'm all right."

She placed a hand on his heart, bent down and kissed him lightly on the forehead. She asked how he was.

"I'm okay," he said.

"You sure?"

"Yeah, just thinking, you know."

"You hungry?"

"A little."

She never asked about his thoughts, letting him instead talk slowly, without pressure. He stood up, pressing first on his good foot for balance, and took her hand. Together they walked through the darkened hallway into the kitchen. She offered him a beer, but he turned it down, honoring his commitment to the others, who had strongly suggested the use of alcohol be curbed.

"Not tonight, baby," he said.

"You think it'll still come, the call?" she asked, calmly.

"Maybe."

She dished up the food, letting the beans and sauce fall carefully over the white rice, then placing the thin steak and onions next to the red and white mound.

"You want a soda?"

"All right."

She poured him some orange soda from a bottle, sat down and dished herself up some of the food. He laughed as he saw her eating, for the moment forgetting the other matter. She ate as much as he did and yet she remained thin and small. He felt like joking about it, but his heart wasn't in it. When their usual banter didn't develop, her face grew concerned, the seriousness making her suddenly seem older.

"You sure everything's all right?" she asked. "Nothing happened, right?"

"No, nothing happened," he said. "It takes time, that's all."

His mouth already dry, he couldn't enjoy the food. He tried to remember the taste of dog, but the memory eluded him. At first he'd rebelled against the idea. However, as the months passed and he no longer felt driven by his purpose in being there, and without realizing it, he felt drawn to the people and began inquiring about it. They had roasted the dog much as they roasted a pig on the island. On the spit it looked no different except that he had found it difficult to look at the head. The eyes bulged out and a pig's did not, so that you couldn't see death in them. That was the thing with death. You could see it in the eyes, that's why you had to close them. It was total horror.

"And you ate it?" Meekins'd said.

"It was pretty good," he'd said, proudly.

"Christ, Maldonado," Meekins said, making a face and running towards the back of the hut. When he came back his face was chalk white from vomiting. "Christ, you people are like fucking slopes or something. You even look like one of them."

Black Thompson and Traynor had laughed, but he just stared at Meekins, noting the way the muscles of his face bulged and receded as he fought the anger, his face growing redder and his eyes crazed. It wasn't until later that night that he recalled Meekins and his pictures of the hunting dogs back home in South Carolina. His laughter was uncontrollable then, and Black Thompson, in his best drill sergeant voice, told him to shut up. When he wouldn't stop laughing, Thompson came over to his bunk.

"Cut out that goddamn barking, Marine," he'd said. "What in the hell, you think this is, boy? What you think you in? A pet shop or the Corps. Huh, boy? Are you a Marine or a poodle?"

He was from Bed-Sty, Thompson. Maldonado had run into him a couple of years back. He was going to college and had gotten married. Smiling, he took off the sun glasses and showed him how they had fixed up his eye. "Me and Sammy Davis, Jr., huh, Sonny? Twenty-one karat glass. Full disability. You think you're the only one knows how to beat the system. Shit." Same old Thompson. Still joking and looking out for the pain.

Carmen had been watching, noting his change in mood.

"Why don't you try eating?" she said.

"I'm not hungry."

"You thinking about the call?"

"Yeah, I guess so. If I knew where I had to go, I'd feel like eating."

"You should anyway. You'll be hungry later."

"Maybe you're right," he said, and made an effort to eat. As usual she was right and he forgot the call for the moment. When they were finished he sat smoking a cigarette and sipping sweet black coffee. He could never get over the size of the cups, so small and thin that he could see the level of the coffee through the china. They were like herself: delicate, small and yet strong.

"Did you read the article?"

"I couldn't get into it."

"Did you try?"

"It doesn't have anything to do with P.R. except that the people were being messed over by the French, right?"

"That's right."

"And the Americans later."

"Right."

"There's nothing else," he said, somberly.

"Maybe afterwards you'll be able to read it. After it's over. You sure you want to go if they call? They said you didn't have to go if you weren't ready."

That was his lie to her.

"I'm ready," he said, looking up at her as she stood near the stove. "I told them I'd do it, but the longer I have to wait the more nervous I'll get."

"Are you scared?"

He nodded and looked away from her. After a few seconds he turned his eyes to her once more.

"And you?"

"Yeah, of course."

"Don't worry," he said. "I can take care of myself."

He said it matter-of-factly, without boasting, but simply to reassure her. He lit another cigarette, remembered that he shouldn't smoke or throw cigarettes down along the way and then the phone rang. He let Carmen answer it. When she returned from the bedroom he immediately knew everything was on.

"It's Romero," she said, her nostrils flaring slightly with the first obvious signs of fear.

"Is he all right?"

"He wants to talk to you."

He stood up, avoiding her eyes, listening to his instincts. Everything seemed far away now as he walked through the dark hallway. He was in a tunnel and it would go on forever. But he felt relief now that the call had come. The anxiety of waiting was gone. In its place, however, he felt the mounting responsibility of the task ahead. He picked up the phone, its lightness pleasing him, feeling comfortable with the surging strength invading his body.

"Mando?" he said.

"Sonny?"

"Yeah, what's happening?"

"The equipment came."

"Everything okay?"

"Sure. Meet me in the restaurant."

"Fifteen minutes?"

"Make it twenty."

"All right. I'll be there."

There was now a long silence. It was as if one minute they had been side by side and the next, moving quickly away through time, the distance increasing with each passing moment. Everything appeared magnified to his senses, his mind expanding outward to take in every sound and smell around him. He heard Romero's voice reiterating the time and then the click of the phone. He was back in Nam again, listening, watching, his heart beating with anticipation, but his mind clear, his eyes seeing everything in detail, his hands holding the rifle loosely and yet securely. Time had stopped and he was on the edge of nothingness. He replaced the receiver and began walking back to the kitchen. Although he didn't want to admit it yet, didn't want to confuse the two events, he felt exactly the same as he did before shooting the boy.

He wondered if the Viet Cong had a casualty report. There certainly would be a casualty report tomorrow. Newspapers, radio, television. Everybody would carry the news, citing the dead and the wounded. There would be plenty. But they wouldn't call it a casualty report, just like the people didn't deal with all the misery in terms of a casualty report. They should, he thought weakly. They really should. The dope addicts who OD, the bums in the street, the pimps and whores, the abandoned children, the women that got beat up by their old men, the people with broken dreams. God, the whole neighborhood was a casualty report. All of them should be listed. And the more he thought about it, the angrier he grew. Every Rivera from Manatí, every Toro from Lares, every Benítez from Luquillo, every Vargas from Barranquitas, every Nieves from Adjuntas, every Martínez from Vieques ... his mind was racing, caught in some mad, turbulent wind which threatened to carry him off ... if he didn't go they would all be on the casualty report ... Pito in the South Bronx, Pupi in the Lower East Side, Papo in los Sures in Brooklyn, Chiqui in Chicago, Baby in Boston, Felito in Philly

... *¡Coño!* He had to go otherwise they'd all be on the casualty report ... And Carmen ... and the babies ... born on the casualty report ...

In the kitchen Carmen was crying softly. Sonny Maldonado stood watching her, his mind already away from the reality of his own life. He wanted to touch her, but knew it would make everything worse.

"It's on, isn't it?" she said, without looking up.

"It's on," he said. "I have to go."

"Will it be bad this time?"

"Yes, very bad."

"Please be careful," she said, turning now and looking pleadingly at him.

"I'll be back tomorrow morning," he said, turning and walking down the hall and out of the apartment, each step, even with his absent foot, filled with renewed certainty about what he must do.

PESO MOSCA

The day Justino Carmona learned that his cousin was dead, the sky was gray and the wind carried a threat of snow. For years he'd been preparing himself for the moment when someone informed him that Eladio, once a Golden Gloves champion, had been found on a rooftop or a hallway. Fortunately, he was spared some of the shame. As he came out of the subway and into the enveloping tenement dusk, Pascual Marrero, a friend, ran out of El Sol de Borinquen, the restaurant where he worked, and stopped him. As soon as Justino saw Pascual's face he knew Eladio was gone. His head felt suddenly light and he began shivering.

"It's Eladio, isn't it?" he said.

Pascual dried his hands on his apron and nodded.

"Please accept my condolences," he said. "I'm sorry."

Justino lowered his head to avoid Pascual's eyes. There was no shock in the news. He'd steeled himself to the scene: the urine-stained pants, the slack face and dry spittle which, like airplane glue on a carelessly built plastic model, collects on the corners of the mouth. He was set to confront the lifeless glazed eyes and the leather-colored skin of Eladio's Taino features, faded as if his face were a discarded woman's handbag, exposed first to rain and then to the sun, making the chemicals which went into its tanning run in ugly discolored streaks. There was, in fact, a sense of relief that Eladio had finally escaped the misery of his life. Funeral arrangements had to be made, but Justino felt as if he'd just completed a job and was about to start on another. He saw himself tightening one last bolt and rolling himself out from under a car, the sweat and grease coming at him in separate smells; he saw himself stand up and head for the washroom to clean up before replacing a busted headlight or connecting some loose wires under a dashboard.

"It's better this way," he said, after a while.

He knew it sounded cruel but it was true. Eladio was too far gone. He also knew the sadness would eventually follow. That's how it was when his father died. Weeks had gone by and then one night, unable to sleep, the torrent of sorrow swept over him. Pascual was now saying the police wanted someone to go to the precinct.

"He didn't have no ID and they said if nobody came they'd have to bury him with the bums," Pascual said, blowing into his ungloved hands and then rubbing his bare arms. When he pressed against the flesh he left white marks against the reddened skin. Justino was thankful Pascual hadn't slipped up and said "other bums." People said things like that without thinking and then felt bad.

"When did it happen?" he asked, not with any great curiosity, but as if it was expected of him.

"Last night, I guess," Pascual said.

"Park Avenue?"

"Yeah, you know. Where they hang out."

Justino asked if he meant the abandoned buildings, but Pascual didn't know.

"Tony and Felix came and told me. They were on their way to work and you were already gone. I was gonna call Doris but I didn't wanna bother her with it."

"That's all right. You sure it was him?"

"Tony said he saw his face when they were putting him into the thing, but that he was bent up funny."

"What thing, the ambulance?"

"No, you know. Those bags."

"He wasn't shot, was he?"

Pascual shook his head and said he didn't think so.

"Felix said there was some white stuff frozen on his jacket. You know, on the side and on the pants."

"White stuff?"

"Yeah, you know. Milk. I guess the guys he was with tried to bring him out of it with milk and it spilled."

Again Justino avoided Pascual's eyes. Pascual said he had to return inside and why didn't he come in and have a cup of coffee. Justino shook his head and Pascual said he understood and offered his condolences again. Justino thanked him and continued down the street. He couldn't feel the cold now. His blood seemed to be itching under his scalp, his throat constricted and dry. Street sounds appeared distant, lights dimmer, shapes larger. He'd tell Doris and then go and find out what the police wanted. He couldn't decide whether he ought to call the funeral home first. Perhaps he should call Metropolitan Hospital or Mount Sinai and see if they'd brought him there. His mind seemed to be traveling in a dozen different directions. Walking in the settling darkness, Justino began recalling Eladio's life. Scenes of their childhood in Cacimar came to him vividly.

They had been inseparable as boys, the two of them running in the grassy hills, flying homemade kites, climbing trees for fruit: *jobo, guanábana, tamarindo, mamey, corazón, guamá, guayaba, mangó.* The sweet smells and bright colors of the countryside, the sounds of voices were still fresh in his mind as if youth had ended only yesterday. Between steps, Justino closed his eyes and he was there again, swimming in the clear mountain pool below the rapids. Eladio's small naked body was lean and brown. He was always the fastest of the boys, the most agile in games, his eyes quick and alive with humor. His hands were like finely carved wood, like a guitarist's hands, delicate, almost feminine. When his hands closed, however, they became hard, heavy weapons.

By the time Eladio was twelve, boys much bigger and older respected him. Challenges to his place in the male hierarchy of the town were dealt with immediately. More often than not, a look was sufficient to make an adversary reconsider his folly. When he was fifteen he'd fought a man. They were at the plaza shining shoes on Saturday morning. Justino was only thirteen but already a head taller than him. Eladio was working on the man's shoes when suddenly the man began cursing and accusing him of staining his pants. When Eladio protested his innocence, the man, a canned goods salesman taking orders in the town, reached down and slapped him. Before anyone knew what had happened, Eladio was up, his fist working rapidly against the man's awkward attempts at defending himself. The altercation was over quickly. When the police showed up, the man, his face badly cut by Eladio's fists and his eyes swelling quickly, told them Eladio had hit him with a rock. Fermín Torres, who owned the movie theater, had watched the incident and came to Eladio's defense. Fermín sponsored the Cacimar baseball club and in his youth had run track at the engineering college in Mayagüez. Eladio's career as a boxer began at that moment.

Within a year he was living outside the capital in the home of one of the best trainers on the island. At sixteen he no longer wanted to attend school. Jobs, other than chopping sugar cane, were hard to come by. He began training full time. The trainer gave him a job in his hardware store in Hato Rey and as he explained the weight of nails and how to mix paint, he talked about boxing, how to tie up someone and still get in a punch or two, the use of the ropes in defensive situations, cutting the ring in half when he was in with a dancer, using his head, both figuratively and literally, and above all, developing pride about his talent. Eladio was just a boy but fight people around the capital immediately recognized his potential as a great fighter. "*Tiene talla de campeón,*" they said knowingly. "He's cut out to be a champ." And they compared him to Sixto Escobar, the exciting bantam weight, who was World Champion from 1936 to 1940 and who gave the island so much to cheer about. Eladio met him and shook his hand. They even posed for photographs together.

"Bantamweight for sure. Wait till he grows," people said.

When the light changed and he was across Third Avenue, Justino slowed down his pace. As he walked in the winter twilight, the icy wind making his face hot and his eyes shed false tears, he recalled the times Eladio had returned to Cacimar.

His body was beginning to show the effects of training, the road work and rope skipping, the endless hours at the bags and in the ring. The natural looseness of the youthful athlete was being replaced by the classic style great boxers develop in their every movement, the confidence which they radiate. Eladio did have all the traits of a champion. Being suddenly the center of attention, however, he began to display a frail shyness which made him smile with embarrassment at mention of his talent. Physically handsome, this made him even more sought after. In the capital, men saw him as a younger brother, and motherly instincts bloomed in even the most hardened and bitter of women who frequented the bars and restaurants where the fight crowd carried on most of its dealings. Whenever he returned to Cacimar, girls and their chaperones flocked to the plaza for their evening *paseos* to smile covertly at Eladio as he stood talking to his friends.

As he continued home, Justino felt suspended between two separate worlds, that of the present and that which he was able to recall so vividly. By the time he arrived at his apartment, his mind was flitting rapidly back and forth from the familiarity of everyday life to those days of glory with Eladio. He opened the door of the tenement, kissed his wife, Doris, and told her about Eladio's death. He didn't expect her to understand how he felt, but she did, just as she had understood everything else which had come their way in twenty years of marriage. Doris crossed herself and asked him if he wanted coffee.

"Yes, I think I'm catching something," he said, feeling the cold for the first time since speaking to Pascual. "It looks like it's gonna snow." As he sat at the kitchen table, his coat still on, he felt suddenly old and a terrible unknown fear gripped him. "Where are the girls?" he said, the fear turning to concern for his daughters, his treasures, still his little girls even though Nancy was in college and Margie was about to graduate from high school.

"They're shopping on Third Avenue," Doris said, the tone of her voice reassuring him of their safety.

"I have to go to the precinct," he said, warming his hands on the coffee cup Doris had placed before him. "There's nobody else, you know. Tito and Victor didn't know him like I did."

"May he rest in peace," Doris said and once more crossed herself without turning from the stove. "We'll say a rosary for him in the house if you want." When Justino did not answer, she turned from the steaming pot of rice and said she'd go down the block and ask Doña Panchita. "She's the best around here," she said.

Justino nodded absently and sipped the sweet coffee. He was lost in thought, his mind pulling him back to those days when he and Eladio were boys.

Eladio had been raised by his parents after Eladio's mother died when he was five. He'd been closer to him than to his brothers Tito, Efraín or Víctor, who were older. He'd been so proud the first time he'd seen Eladio fight in the ring. It was the finals of the Golden Gloves, although they weren't yet called Guantes Dorados. They'd left in the morning, he and his father and his brothers. Everyone in Cacimar knew Eladio was fighting for the championship that night.

On the way to the capital Justino sat on the bus and followed each rise and fall in the road, the asphalt canopied by the red foliage of the *flamboyán* trees. He was mesmerized by the dizzying precipices, which plunged to tiny valleys, stretching like a green carpet in the distance. They changed buses in Caguas and then in Río Piedras. When they arrived at Plaza de Colón in old San Juan, his father pointed out El Teatro Tapia and then took them to see El Morro and San Cristóbal, the Spanish forts. Later on they boarded the ferry to Cataño. The spray of salt water coated his face as he watched pelicans diving for fish. On the other side they had a lunch of *jueyes*, the fine blue crabs of the coast. They'd come back and gone to the museum and zoo in Luis Muñoz Rivera Park and walked around the Condado section. The Normandie Hotel, in those days the only hotel in the area, resembled a ship sailing into the palm trees. Sixto Escobar Stadium, where he was to fight, was next to the hotel. People were already lining up to purchase tickets for the fights. As the moment when Eladio was to enter the ring approached, Justino grew more excited, the feeling of pride swelling in him.

Eladio never reached bantam weight. He remained 5 foot-3 inches and his weight stayed at 112 pounds. But he was magnificent that night, dressed in his red boxing trunks and high shoes, his body slender but muscular, the upper part carved like the finely turned bedposts made of the rich mahogany which was so much in vogue those days. Tears came into Justino's eyes when the band played the national anthem of Puerto Rico at the beginning of the fight card. He stood proudly with his right hand at his heart while he sang with the crowd.

> *La tierra de Borinquen donde he nacido yo*
> *Es un jardín florido de mágico esplendor.*
> *Un cielo siempre nítido le sirve de dosel*
> *Y dan arrullos plácidos las olas a sus pies.*

The emotion was even greater when they announced Eladio's name and he came out of his corner, dancing and moving his hands and feet like a professional. The stadium became suddenly still. In the distance, beyond the center field fence and the darkness, one could hear the waves of Escambrón Beach. Eladio came to the center of the ring and listened courteously to the referee's instructions. He returned to his corner and, holding on to the top strand of the ropes, squatted several times, stood up and made the sign of the cross with his right glove. When the bell rang he came out of his corner dancing on the balls of his feet. The crowd, as if sensing greatness, exploded wildly into applause, the noise rising above the brilliant lights of the stadium to be lost in the starry night.

All around Justino, people bobbed and weaved as they followed Eladio's movements. In a chorus they urged him on. "*La zurda, Ladín. Un gancho. Noquéalo con la zurda.*" They were in a frenzy, screaming for Eladio to throw his already famous left hook, which had knocked out four opponents in the competition. Eladio seemed unconcerned with the crowd. Instead, like a cat amusing itself with a mouse whose fate had been sealed, he toyed with the other fighter, a wild-swinging left-handed kid, badly trained and out of his class. Eladio would let the kid come at him, his fist clawing the air as if he were trying to climb a wall, and Eladio would dance back, jabbing at the unprotected head. "*Le dió en la cara,*" people shouted, implying that Eladio's blows were meant to be insulting. "*Si le da bien lo mata,*" others said: "One good punch and he'll kill him."

In the second round Eladio proved there was pure steel in his fists. Halfway through the round Eladio went to work in earnest. He jabbed four times with his left, crossed his right to the head and, feigning a jab, hooked off of it and knocked out the left-hander cleanly. After the kid was counted out, Eladio raised his fists triumphantly and danced around the ring. The corner people had to chase him. When they caught him they lifted him up on their shoulders. The crowd couldn't contain itself: "Ladín, Ladín, Ladín," they shouted, using Eladio's nickname.

Later that evening all of them—Justino and his father and brothers, Eladio and Fermín Torres and the trainer Cuco Enríquez, and the corner people—went to El Nilo Restaurant. Inside there was a stone fountain with large goldfish. The place smelled, not like the restaurants in Cacimar, but like the food rich people must eat. His father let Justino drink a half a glass of beer, even though he was only fourteen. He ate a grilled pork sandwich with lettuce and tomato and later ice cream. Eladio wore a smile so infectious and wide that people at other tables began asking waiters who he was. Cuco Enríquez said they were looking at a future World Champion.

All the way home, in a rented car, the night air of the mountains crisp and intoxicating and the dark sky sprinkled with stars, Justino could still hear the crowd chanting Eladio's name and see him dancing, his head bobbing and his gloved hands working intricate patterns of attack. Halfway to Cacimar, Justino fell asleep against his father's shoulder and dreamt of traveling with Eladio all over the world when he was a champion.

The next day was Saturday and Justino bought a copy of *El Imparcial*. He went around showing his friends a picture of Eladio standing above his vanquished opponent. That afternoon Eladio came home with his entourage. He said he was turning professional. Fermín Torres told Justino's father that Eladio had a bright future as a boxer. The entire family went to city hall, where the mayor and the police captain shook Eladio's hand and congratulated him on being a credit to his family and the town of Cacimar.

Justino finished the last of his coffee, zipped up his jacket and headed for the door. Doris stopped him and made him take a scarf and gloves.

"I'll fix up the altar for the rosary," she said.

"Yes, use the picture of Eladio when he turned professional," Justino said. "That's how I want to remember him."

Justino walked the six blocks to the police station. Once there he spent nearly an hour reassuring a bored, red-faced detective that he was Eladio's cousin. Hating the impersonality of the place, Justino grew morose. He asked to speak to the officers who'd found Eladio, but was told they'd gone off duty at four o'clock that afternoon.

"You're gonna have to make a positive ID, pal," the detective said. "Down at the morgue."

Justino signed a form, took a slip of paper given to him by another officer and headed downtown. All the way there, as he rode the subway, he continued to recall scenes from Eladio's life.

After Justino came to New York he'd lost touch with Eladio. Periodically, he'd get news through relatives, but he didn't hear from Eladio directly until he showed up at his apartment a couple of years after Justino and Doris had gotten married. Things hadn't gone well for Eladio. He'd fallen in with a bad crowd, lost a couple of important fights, was dropped by Fermín Torres, and he had gone down in ranking. He was broke and about the only need fight people on the island had for him was to serve as a sparring partner for younger boxers. At the age of twenty-four Eladio was washed up. Rather than the almost feminine shyness he developed after his initial success, Eladio was now a cocky man of the world, talking fast and pretending to smile self-assuredly.

"I came north to see if I could make a few dollars," he'd said as he guzzled beer at Florindo's Bar on Lexington Avenue.

"Boxing?" Justino had asked.

"No, that's kid's stuff. I have some connections up here. What I'd like to do is open a bar. Like the one in Cayey that belongs to Pedro Montañez. You know, with all his boxing pictures and trophies. That appeals to people. They go for that up here. There's probably a lot of *jíbaros* around who remember me from the ring."

Justino looked at Eladio's eyes and saw uncertainty in them. He also noticed a bit of scar tissue, but it was Eladio's doubt which always remained with him. Years later Justino found out from his brother Tito that Eladio had gone into a main event bout without having trained adequately and was badly beaten. "But I think he was already scared before that," Tito had said, adding that Eladio had gotten a young girl in trouble and her father had threatened to kill him if he didn't marry her. That was the reason Eladio had come to New York.

Nothing had seemed to work for Eladio. His drinking became heavier. In the harsh atmosphere of the bars in El Barrio he soon became the butt of jokes whenever he spoke about boxing. Word got around that he'd been an amateur champion and a promising professional, but few people believed that the scrawny, sad-faced Eladio was anything more than another loser shooting off his mouth. Within six months Eladio had disappeared. Nobody knew what had happened to him, whether he'd gone back to the island or drifted into the anonymity of life in New York. Justino had expected to run into him working in the kitchen of a restaurant, his fine talented hands submerged to the wrists in soap suds.

Two years later he showed up looking terrible, but smiling from ear to ear. His English had improved and in spite of his physical condition and seedy clothing, he seemed happy. Some of his humility had returned. Justino imagined it came from the realization that one has to allow some dreams to be shattered in order to survive. He asked Eladio how things were going and Eladio told him he'd gone upstate to pick produce with people from the island. He said it was pretty good work and that the company flew the *jíbaros* up for the season. He added that he was thinking of returning to the island and building himself a house in Cacimar. When Justino pressed him about the work, he said there wasn't much money in it, but that at least there was plenty of fresh air and less trouble, and in the off season he did odd jobs and taught kids to box.

Justino was pleased by the tone of Eladio's voice. It seemed to carry a new found hope and resolve to fight on. He invited Eladio home to eat. Eladio played with Nancy and Margie and later, when the girls were in bed and Doris was sewing in the kitchen, he pulled out his wallet and showed Justino pictures of his own children. "Twins," he said. "Gaspar and Mercedes, after Papá and Mamá," he said, smiling proudly when he mentioned Justino's parents. "*Me casé con una morena americana,*" he'd said, almost in a whisper, explaining why his English was so good, but somehow apologizing for marrying an American Black woman.

He came and went many times in the ensuing years, on each occasion revealing another part of himself to Justino. One time he was gone an entire year. When he returned there was a deep, ugly scar on his cheek. He wouldn't talk about it and made jokes about the other guy. His face had grown tired and old before its time and he was drinking heavily again. As if he had been caught in a whirlpool whose bottom were hell, Eladio's life continued to spiral downward. After his wife ran off with his children, Eladio began hanging out around El Barrio again. Within a year he was using heroin and whenever he came to see Justino it was always for a handout or with a scheme for making money in a hurry, claiming then that he was giving up his habit. Justino saw Eladio for the last time four days prior to the news of his death. He weighed no more than ninety pounds, due to the life of the streets, the hustling, the wheeling and dealing, the illness of dirty needles and damp sleeping places and fears of being caught without the next fix. Eladio was a ghost of his former self.

It was nearly eight o'clock when Justino entered the city morgue and handed the guard the slip of paper from the police. He was escorted through a set of double doors and told to sit down. He had expected a certain somberness to be present among the people. Instead, he found the same lack of concern present in any official department of the city. When the guard spoke to him, he felt as he did at the post office or as he had at the police station. There seemed to be, if not a tiredness to people's movement, then a resignation to their fate. It was as if resenting the insignificance of their lives, they saw the limited power the system had given them and were ready to enforce the most minute of ordinances in order to feel worthwhile. To smile understandingly, to show the least sign of compassion for another human being, was to capitulate, to give into the impotency of the job.

"You ready?" said the attendant, a sallow, middle-aged man. Justino nodded. "There's some complications," the attendant said, motioning him to follow. "You his brother?"

"Cousin."

"Well, we gotta do an autopsy and we need permission to saw the body."

Justino didn't understand the man. He'd always had trouble with the words "sew" and "saw" and couldn't imagine why they'd have to suture Eladio.

"Was he cut bad?" he asked.

The attendant said he hadn't been cut and continued down the hall. Justino caught up to him and asked why they had to sew up Eladio. He made a motion as if he were working a needle and thread. The attendant stopped, made a sawing motion and Justino shook his head and then understood.

"Saw, like wood?" he said.

"Yeah, like that, mister. He was frozen stiff when they found him. Maybe six hours, maybe more. You wanna follow me."

They entered a tiled room with lockers built into the wall. Justino recognized the place from movies. The attendant looked at his clipboard, found the right number and pulled on the locker door. The metal slab slid out and the attendant pulled the sheet back. Justino had not noticed the shape of the body until the sheet was removed. Eladio's face was barely visible. He was on his side, his small body bent grotesquely. It was as if someone had taken a rag doll and folded it forward at the waist, or as if someone had forced Eladio to touch his forehead to his knees. His hands, his once beautifully sculpted hands were gnarled, frozen claws attempting to vainly grasp his feet. Horrified by the sight, Justino stared at the gray form that had once been his cousin. When the attendant finally asked him if the body was that of the person he had known as his cousin, Justino wanted to scream that it wasn't, but he said it was and signed the forms.

"What happened?" he asked once they were outside the room. His voice was choked with suppressed emotion. "Why is he like that?"

"Mister, I already told you," said the attendant. "He froze."

"Why?" Justino said helplessly.

"I don't know that one. I don't cut up no bodies. That's for the medical examiner. You gotta sign something else so we can saw him up and find out what happened for sure."

"With a saw?" Justino asked again.

The word had no meaning. He kept thinking of Doris darning his socks or mending a dress on the sewing machine. Only when he thought of the Spanish word *serrucho* did it all make sense, and then a chill went through him and the small hairs at the back of his neck felt as if some large awful insect were crawling on him.

"It's a surgical saw," said the attendant. "Same one they use for amputation in a hospital. You gonna sign?"

Justino felt faint and was having trouble focusing his eyes. He scribbled his name on the form and the attendant said the body could be picked up by the funeral home anytime after noon the next day and that if it wasn't picked up within twenty-four hours the city would have to bury it in Potter's Field.

All the way home and that night as he lay awake Justino thought about Eladio: his twisted, pain-wracked body lying on the cold aluminum surface, soul-less, empty of feeling, empty of dreams and thoughts. In the morning he called the garage where he worked and explained that there had been a death in the family. He then went to the bank, withdrew most of the money he'd saved during the year and went to the funeral home to make arrangements. The wind blew cold all day. Towards sundown the sky turned red. When Justino returned to the funeral home that evening, Eladio was laid out in a suit, his face powdered, the grimace of death cosmetically replaced by the straight-lipped resignation of eternal sleep, his voice silenced forever to the pain.

After sitting in front of the casket for several minutes, Justino suddenly got up. He felt angry and was certain that if he remained in the room he'd grab Eladio by the lapels and begin shaking him. The funeral director, standing in the doorway to the chapel, asked him if everything was as he had ordered it. Justino nodded and asked what had happened to Eladio. The funeral director, a solemn and polite man, did not want to discuss it. He said it was against the funeral home's policy. Justino insisted.

"I have a right to know," he said, the words choking him. "The police didn't tell me anything and those people downtown were even worse."

The man coughed discreetly and asked Justino to please lower his voice. He motioned Justino into his office and asked him to sit down. When he was seated the funeral director apologized and said he could lose his job, but that he understood how Justino felt. He asked if Justino was aware that Eladio was a drug user. Justino said it was pretty obvious.

"But they had to ... you know," Justino said, painfully, making a sawing motion with his hand. "What happened?"

The funeral director said all they had been told was that Eladio was found in that position, and that he had died of an overdose of heroin. He added that the cold hadn't killed Eladio, but that he guessed that whoever was with him must've tried to revive him by walking him around. When that failed, he said, they probably got scared and sat him against some garbage cans and he slid in. He said it sounded crazy, but that it was the only thing he could figure out.

"In a garbage can?" said Justino, recalling Eladio's body at the morgue. "It isn't possible."

"He was a small man," said the funeral director.

"Yes," said Justino sadly, adding, as if to justify the indignity, that Eladio had been a boxer at one time. "Fly weight," he said.

"*¿Peso mosca?*" asked the funeral director.

"*Sí, peso mosca.*"

"Please accept my condolences."

Justino stood up and thanked the funeral director for his *pésame*, his condolences. He returned to the chapel, took one more look at Eladio and then went into the street. The wind had died down and light snow had begun falling, coating the street and sidewalks with a glistening, thin sheet of white. On the corner a group of boys was already busy trying to make snow balls. Across the street, at the record shop, a young woman was hanging a garland of Christmas lights in the window. Justino walked through the crystal-like flakes and, for the first time in his life, was afraid of dying.

FISHING

There he was—the one and only William Ballester of "The Yankee Hornpipe Ensemble," all decked out in faded jeans and flowered shirt, riding in a limousine to attend a funeral at the age of thirty, leaving the crowded city streets and then the highway, coming to rest among the tall trees and stone somewhere in Long Island. Memories of memories of another island spun themselves anew like silken silver threads. Words of the other language which people called Spanish, but which had meant much more, drifted in and out of his mind like fleeting clouds on a breezy summer day. And his mother, through her tears, saying, "It isn't right. He was a good man, a decent man. You could've dressed appropriately."

William Ballester, among vines of many colors, playing a broken-hearted lute and flute somewhere in space, suspended by harp strings, the red and blue and yellow lights flying in his face like cosmic dust. And he had only gone fishing with his father once. It had been long ago when tumbling down a hill was the only requirement for existence. Long ago, long ago, he was a child, as was his father before him, as was his own son, so on and so on—the acid no longer an experience but a reality as large as the word "spic," which no amount of polish could erase, this in spite of the lightness of his skin, the flaxen hair and blueness of his eyes. Yes, his father had been a child, and he'd left long ago for good, and soon he would follow as would his son in his due time. The rite, this funeral, belonged to him, the man-boy, sailor-poet, and not to the man inside the casket; it belonged to the memory of his father, who would've wanted music and laughter and mixed-up talk.

He was a fisherman, his father was, and a good one, too, tra-la, tra-la. Over the waves and through the storm, the sails spread open to the wind, his ship a flying thing, he dreaming he was Roberto Cofresí, pirate, defender of the truth when truth meant a cutlass to the throat and nightly raids on Spanish ships. Spinning a tale, building a dream around him so that merchant marine meant nothing.

He'd be gone for weeks, months at a time, and on his return the questions in his hands were dream-stuff. India, Japan, Madagascar and the Ivory Coast. Red,

66

Blue, Orange and Yellow on the map. He saw them with his eyes, all a-sparkle he saw them. Treasure. Then he'd tumble down the hill, smelling the grass as if for the very first time, and at the bottom his father would pick him up in his arms and toss him in the air and catch him as he flew. His face was tanned, weathered tan, his green eyes deep and smiling as if they knew something but wouldn't tell anyone, and when he spoke his mustache spread like black silk across his handsome face.

"Hello, Bill," he'd say, the Spanish surrounding the words so that sentences became songs. "Did you sleep well last night, my good companion friend? Butterflies in your sleep and flowers at your window pane. A whale is a mammal, or didn't you know?" Talking crazy so that each word was a soap bubble, breaking before he could capture it, the sun gleaming on its nonsurface for only a moment and the letters gone, the sound tinkling, the meaning lost. "Who do you know that I haven't seen or heard?" he'd say. "The wind? Tell me, or I'll crab you where it hurts, I will, young Bill, Guillermo Ballester, *mi hijo, taíno del nido de Huracán, poeta de entrañado amor, de noche de amapolas y sueños de alelí,*" he'd say. And then they'd laugh, climb up again and tumble down the hill in front of their house, which was all white and faced the sea, a mile or so down from the lighthouse where they had moved to get away from the slums and gangs and dope, but mostly because his mother was Irish, black Irish, with eyes bluer and deeper than the sea and hair like midnight.

It was all Papa those years before he left.

Night began by candlelight, and the fire danced and crackled while the foghorns wept.

"When's he coming back, Mama?"

"Soon, Billy," she'd say, and he could tell she wanted to cry. She was so beautiful there by the fire with the candlelight playing on her black hair as if it were yellow rain. Did you ever see anything like it even in a dream? He had, and it wasn't pretty because he knew there was something wrong and couldn't tell what and he couldn't wake up since his eyes were open and he couldn't look away.

But his father never came back after they went fishing and didn't catch anything except an itty-bitty, which was a fish of very little size. His father had said the itty-bitty missed his mother and threw him back into the Brooklyn Sea.

"It's good and proper to do so, Billy," he'd said. "Ashes to ashes and dust to dust, if you miss the octopus then wait for the bus. *¿Entiendes?*" His father laughed, then sung a song about a mermaid and her lover having fish for babies. His voice sounded like a clarinet, so hollow and reedy and deep. And he was so handsome, dark like a sea gypsy wandering the earth in search of who knew what, singing so you could never tell things hurt. "What will you be when you grow up, young Bill?" he'd ask. "Not a sailor, I hope. Not a sailor or a tailor or a failure not. There's nothing worse than a man content," he'd say, holding a mug aloft, beer foam specks sparkling on his mustache like the first snow outside your window.

In the summer there was no one for miles around, and he'd watch the sea each day, rain or shine for hours at a time, so that the sky seemed to have breakers of its own and porpoises swam in it just to deceive him into believing he was sitting upside down on a rock below the house. He was never sick or lonely then. Mama baked fresh bread every day, but after Papa didn't come back, Bill had to walk to the grocery store down the beach and inland to buy bread. She wrote letters at night, and in the morning he'd take them to the post office, and people asked him how he was. They always looked like they had bad news but never said so.

"Where have you gone, young Bill, Guillermo Ballester," he'd ask on his return from the sea. "*¿Adónde, pájaro verde y azul de alas de oro y pico de tul?* I've been to there and back to see the king and brought a mile of string. Where have *you* been?"

"Nowhere, Papa."

"Nowhere. My Lord. Pity me, pity me. Do you know what makes up stars? Tell me then, if you will, young Bill, and I'll reward you glad."

"I don't know, Papa."

"Sing me a song and I'll give you a dime, young Bill, Guillermo Ballester," saying his name with the jet sound and not like everyone else who pronounced it like l's, making it sound like ballast, which his father explained and read from the big dictionary kept open on a stand near the fireplace: 1) any heavy substance, as sand, stone, etc., laid in the hold of a vessel or in the car of a balloon to steady it; 2) gravel or broken stone laid down as a stabilizer for a railroad bed; 3) that which gives stability to character, morality, etc.; and he said it was as well pronounced in English, since he was then the man who did all three, added weight to the world and was of such fine character and blood that anyone would be glad to have him for a friend anywhere in English and in Spanish both. And then he'd grow serious and say the name was *Catalán*, and *Ballester* meant archer and talked about crossbows, his words flying slowly from his lips like lonely sea gulls against a graying sky. "And it's the name for a bird. *Falziot* in the *Catalán* tongue and *martinete* on the Island of Enchantment where you and I will go someday and live as pirates. So sing me a song, young Bill, Guillermo Ballester, my son, and on to Cacimar we'll go."

And then he sang "Jack and Jill went up the hill," and his father laughed and clutched him to his chest, his eyes like green fire; and taking his mother in his arms so she seemed lost in him, he was so big and strong, he danced the two of them around the room. Those days she danced and laughed with his father, and at night he could hear them talking to each other so softly it sounded like the sea was weeping. Did you ever dream you were a bird and flew forever? That's what falling asleep was like back then.

The day his father returned from Borinquen in the Caribbean Sea, he was eight or nine, he didn't remember which, it was so long ago. He'd never been to Borinquen because he hadn't become a sailor or a tailor, although some said he'd failed in spite of his father's warning, having chosen to build songs to play and sing. But he knew the location of the Island even then, thought something had happened there, and finally it hadn't mattered where the trouble began.

He saw the ship early in the morning and knew it was his father's ship. It was way out like a fading bird in a painting, and he watched it all the way until the sea was lost beneath the hill, and Pepe and Rosita, his friends, said good morning, and he was back on the road to wait for the school bus. He'd wanted to turn back and tell his mother it was his father's ship, but she knew it, he guessed. All morning he'd wanted to run out of school and catch a train to the docks in the "dirty city," as his mother called South Brooklyn. Instead he did sums and read out loud, and Mrs. Cavendish said it was a good thing he had a brain because then he could go on to college and make something of himself.

When he came home his father was there, sipping tea and feeling like the world had been rained on and everyone drowned except him. His mother was standing by the window looking at the sea, her arms clasped to herself as if she were cold. When his father saw him come into the room he jumped from his chair, and Bill, seeing his father, dropped his books and ran to him. Up in the air he went so that his hair brushed the ceiling.

"There you be, young Bill," he said. "And what news bring you from school, hey, hey?"

He'd laughed and asked his father if he'd brought him a gift.

"Aye, aye, I brought ye a gold compass, lad," he said, talking like Mr. Molloy at the grocery store.

"Oh, Papa, no kidding?"

"Not one ounce, more or less. Belonged to the King of Portugal in 1743 or thereabouts somewhere."

"Let me see it. Please let me see it."

"Not before you sing a song for old times sake. What do you say?"

"I'll sing a song, Papa."

"Don't tease him so, Bill," his mother said.

"I'm not teasing him, Chris. He's got a fine voice, and I like to hear him sing. There's no crime in that."

"I'll sing, Mama. Don't worry."

"*Canta, ruiseñor de mi infancia. Canta, sombra de mi corazón,*" his father had said, and he had somehow understood in spite of hearing him for the first time in three months.

And he sang "Oh, beautiful, for spacious skies," which he had learned the previous week in school. When he was finished his father clapped and his mother, tears in her eyes, asked if he wanted a buttered muffin and some tea. His father went to his sea bag and told him he must close his eyes. He waited, swaying and swaying like the mast of a ship at anchor, and then the compass was in his hands. He couldn't open his eyes because it was like being in a dream, and when a dream was good, it was always sad if he woke up too soon.

"All right, open 'em up, young Bill. Behold a wonder of magic and science before your very eyes."

It was a beautiful thing, the compass, about the size of a baseball, the needle jumping with the slightest movement, pointing one way and then another as he moved, the fine polished brass glinting softly in the sunlight. He couldn't sleep that night, feeling for the compass to make sure it was still by his side. His father and mother had talked a long time, and their voices were not soft but whispered as if they didn't want to wake him.

He didn't go to school the next day, and his father said he'd take him down to the sea to fish. His mother said he should've gone to school.

"He's my son too, woman," his father said. "Or do you have more news for me?"

His mother did not answer, and he and his father left. They went down to the place where the surf pounded the rocks, and the spray was not wet but salty on his face.

"Do you miss me when I'm gone, Billy?" his father asked, his words faintly accented, as if he had taken another step in mastering the language. He answered that he did, and his father didn't say anything more until they caught the itty-bitty fish they had to throw back. After he finished singing about the mermaid, his father looked so sad it seemed as if the light had gone out of his eyes.

"It's good to have friends, isn't it, Billy?"

"Yes, Papa."

"Do you have many friends?"

"No, Papa. Just Pepe and Rosita from Puerto Rico. I teach them English and they teach me Puerto Rican."

"Spanish."

"Spanish. They have no father, Papa. I told them you could be their father, if they wanted."

"And what did they say?"

"They didn't understand. Pepe's a little deaf, and Rosita's very shy."

"Did they ever come up to the house?"

"Just once. Mama gave us bread and jam, but they had to go home right away and help their mother. She cleans for the people in the big house on the other side of the dunes."

"Visitors are a wonderful thing. Everyone gets lonely living out here."

"Papa?"

"Yes, Billy."

"If you went away and never came back, would I need another father?"

His father didn't say anything. He turned to the sea, took a deep breath, and tried to start another song but couldn't.

"Sure you would," he said after a while. "Who'd look after you and your Mama?"

"Pepe and Rosita look after each other *and* their mother."

"That's a different story," he said, smiling. "Mrs. Alvarez is used to being alone ... " He stopped speaking and the sadness returned to his eyes. "Did you know your mother played the piano?"

"She said the salt was no good for a piano."

"She's right."

"Papa, is Mr. Sanderson a good man?"

"He's a very good man," he said without hesitation.

"He comes to visit and brings flowers and talks about his music students. I'm learning to play his guitar."

The sea had grown angry. It spit like a cat, its fur standing and the roaring deep in its chest as if it wanted to kill. Rain began falling, and the sky was suddenly gray. They'd gone up the hill without any fish.

At supper time his father and mother wouldn't talk to each other, the silence heavier and louder than the storm outside. The next morning, just as the sun began to come out of the sea, his father came to his bed to say goodbye. He kissed his father and held his face close to his chest, smelling how clean and how much like the sea he was.

"Goodbye, Billy," he said. "See you next time around. Maybe I'll bring you a piece of the moon sometime, my son, Bill, Guillermo Ballester. *Adiós.*"

"Please don't go, Papa."

"I have to, Bill. My ship's leaving today. Go back to sleep, and have a dream for me."

He was gone then, and he never saw him again, never heard his sing-song English-Spanish dreams. And today, among the faded tombstones, William Ballester of "The Yankee Hornpipe Ensemble," electronic rock group on the ascent, was asked by his own son if Grandpa Sanderson was a good man. And he answered that he was indeed a very good man.

"Will he ever come back?"

"No, he won't be back, Bill," he said. "He's dead and buried, and he won't come back."

"Why then so many flowers?" he asked, talking crazy, so that the words hung there like window bells, echoing forever in the wind, his son's eyes far away, dreaming, the world becoming vast before him and time not pausing once.

"I don't know, Bill, my son, Guillermo Ballester."

THE EBONY TOWER

Lou Torres finished correcting the last of the English 101 exams, stood up and stretched his still lithe six-foot frame. After looking at his watch, he locked his office and went down the steps of the tower which served to house the Communications Department of the college. The buildings, raw concrete and glass, set in the clearing of a wooded area in Nassau County in western Long Island, gave the campus an odd architectural appearance. As if a giant child had been left to play with multi-shaped blocks and had arranged them in what he understood to be symmetry of design, the buildings slashed and intercepted the noonday sun to create spectacular geometric shadows on the ground.

As he crossed the plaza surrounded by the buildings, each with its own tower, two thoughts struggled for dominance in Torres' mind. One thought was that of his son's graduation the following day. The other concerned a young woman student. While his son's graduation provided him some measure of pride and accomplishment, the upcoming phone call to the student made him slightly nauseated, as though he were about to commit an unpleasant act. Neither of the two thoughts would win out as a clear sign of his existence. Quite different from each other, the acts would be performed as expediencies for survival. As was his habit when confronted with difficulties, Torres reached into his memories of more pleasant times.

As he walked he reflected on his words at his first faculty meeting almost eight years before. Employing the rhetorical gift inherited from his storefront-preacher father, Torres had made his presence in the school felt immediately. Like a magnificent black hawk swooping down on its prey, he tore at the apathy of his white colleagues and at the impotent nationalism of his black ones.

Perhaps, he began, someone like myself, who, although black in color, shares a European background with many of you, can best speak to the issue at hand. The State University, in designing this college, intended for us to literally abscond into ivory towers. You must not for one moment assume that phenomena around you occur randomly. Unconscious as it might be, the powers who so diligently devised the plans for this institution meant to lull us, all of us, into complacency.

72

The stark reality of those concrete towers means only one thing. And let me parenthesize briefly for the benefit of my white colleagues. Make no mistake. This is a Black institution. Ivory is for white and ebony for blacks. For the gray concrete of those towers, buffeted by the elements and the passage of time, will turn black and rather than becoming ivory towers, they will be transformed into ebony towers and in them will we carry out our mission.

But I have a word of caution for my Black brothers and sisters. Do not for one moment think that the concept of the ebony tower has its origin, or derives its inspiration from caucasoid culture, or for that matter is a Black replica of the ivory tower.

As he walked, Lou Torres thought about the differences between white and black America and wasn't sure if they were not one and the same, at least in attitudes. The Africans he'd met and spoken with certainly thought so. But eight years ago, when he'd come to the college, the difference had been quite clear. There had been some applause at his observation and he'd continued.

The ebony tower is no place for cotton-linted, fuzzy-headed niggers to hide themselves so they don't have to cope with the intellectual challenges faced today by the Third World. The ebony tower, however, is the place for the responsible Black man and woman to aspire to, and from which each day, he and she must descend to walk among his brothers and sisters to teach and inspire them. It is the place from which each and everyone of us must go forth into the community to relearn those elements on which the Black experience is based. It is the place to which we must return to examine ourselves and our failings as educators and as Black men and women.

So let us not quibble about the architectural failings of our institutions. Let us instead give the passage of time its inescapable due and direct ourselves to more relevant matters. For while we sit here depleting our energies in useless debate and antagonism, war rages in Southeast Asia, drought threatens the African continent, the Third World is in political turmoil, and in here, the richest country in the world, children of all colors go hungry and their minds stagnate for want of guidance. Let us determine to go forth from this day and do nothing less than educate.

The last sentence had been delivered solemnly, his rich baritone rising, then falling so the words seemed to linger, their harmonics hanging above the crowd of some one hundred faculty members gathered in the auditorium. Torres experienced the intoxicating effect created when many bodies become one mind, and truth, if not captured, is at least glimpsed for a moment. As he sat down he felt euphoric and filled with new power. The applause went on for a while and several of his new colleagues stood up to cheer him. He recalled basking in the atmosphere he'd created and then becoming aware of Elizabeth Anderson from American Studies at his side. She touched his hand and as he turned he saw in her eyes profound understanding and appreciation for his courage in speaking out.

The touch, the look and later the inevitable cup of coffee established the beginning of their affair, conducted at first clandestinely and away from the campus. And yet, as he walked in the late spring sunlight, he knew that thoughts of his past triumphs inevitably led him to examine his failings. The thoughts came to him unbidden, pushing upward, surfacing and forcing him to bend humiliatingly to their truth. Towards the end, more than two years later, when everyone at the school knew and accepted their weakness, and everything in each of them had been left injured and his hatred for everything white had been vented on her, the love and hate so intertwined that their humanity appeared grotesque and misshapen, Elizabeth Anderson from Millersville, Iowa, PhD from the University of Chicago, had finally admitted to herself that they had used each other. She left the school, shamed by the experience. He, on the other hand, had remained to do penance, his Black power no longer believable, except to the uninitiated, star-gazing student whose sole criterion for respect was attention.

In front of the school, awaiting the shuttle to the train station and his return trip to New York City, Torres felt disturbingly out of place. Several students greeted him but he was aware, in returning their greeting, of an increasing and fatalistic resignation to his fate. He felt that his color, his degrees, his command of language and knowledge of literature had become transparent, and all eyes now focused on his true self. Time had passed him by, and somehow those days of the late 60's and 70's, with their issues and demonstrations and militant spirit, had taken their toll on him and he was today no more than a museum piece, a curio, an exotic antique left in someone's attic to collect dust.

The breakup with Elizabeth had been a nightmare, further complicated by Walter's intrusion. Walter David Torres, his bright child, tall like himself, intelligent, sharp-featured, in his first year of pre-med, came down on him one summer evening, confronting his hypocrisy. He'd just left Elizabeth Anderson's apartment after another argument and had driven fast across the Triborough Bridge to his home in Queens, the place where Walter and Bonita had been raised and where he had taken refuge from his struggles with his blackness back in East Harlem, asking continuously of himself why he had to exist between two worlds, hating his father and mother for creating a hybrid, never wanting to accept his identity as a Black spic.

Walking on 116th Street and Lexington Avenue in full daylight with all the Black faces who drifted down from Harlem to shop under the elevated tracks of the Park Avenue Market, he would look at the white woman who was his mother and accept the fact that he was a *halfbreed* (he'd heard the epithet in westerns and a surge of pleasure always invaded his soul, as if in the word he had at last found respite). He was a halfbreed not only in parentage, but in culture, feeling then the tugging of his parents and their wretched island, their diminutive hometown universe of Cacimar memories, clashing violently with the ever present promise that was America.

He recalled how later, after his Army experiences, when in anger he decided to attend college in the South, he began to ease himself out of the dilemma. Hopelessly in love with a light-skinned Louisiana girl, he sat for hours in the warm evening air, listening to her soft drawl as she coaxed him out of himself by talking about her own French and Spanish background, treating the Black issue as if it were a humorous accident and not something to wear in disgrace.

"Great-great-grandmamá Martine Pelletier started it all when she fell in love with a mulatto, Granville Del Castillo, a gambler. She was a dancer from Paris and he was the son of a ship captain who had bought a Black girl to bring back to Spain. The ship captain was shot in a duel in New Orleans, but the Black girl, Lucille Coleman, was already *encinta* with his child. The man with whom Captain Del Castillo dueled was Harrison Granville, who carried Lucille off, then abandoned her before she gave birth. I suppose she wanted to give the boy the best of both men, so she named him Granville Del Castillo and that's who great-great-grandmamá Martine took up with twenty-five years later."

The story, whether fact or fancy, hadn't much mattered and Torres had allowed himself to become enraptured by her, loving her manner, her delicate movements so different from those of the tacky-haired, rough-talking, big-assed mamas of his high school days, dancing close at fish jumps, drinking wine and smoking *yerba*, feeling cool in wide pants with thirty inch cuffs and garish pink and black shirts and hair pressed slick with Royal Crown, riding the "A" train to Birdland and Charlie Parker and Dizzy Gillespie bop.

He was down South, away, lost in the Blackness, a new Blackness, a pure, non-defensive Blackness where for once he felt acceptance and didn't have to explain his last name and say his father and mother were from the Caribbean, never mentioning Puerto Rico because that would again bring up the problem, and the impotent rage would rise in him again.

And now Walter, his son, sprung from his loins and into those of Charlene Didier, octoroon Louisiana creole, slim and the color of honey, hair so black and wavy, combed out, good hair to run his hands through as he had his mother's when he volunteered to brush it while she waited for his brother, Ronald, to come in from the street, the dope turning Ronald's mouth down into a grimace of self-hatred. He brushed his mother's hair, long and sleek, and hated his own *pasita*, a raisin, as his mother called his kinky hair, as all Puerto Rican mothers with kinky-haired children called it; a little raisin it was and he could never put the two together, in spite of growing up bilingual—raisin being the tiny, sugary fruit and *pasita* the tightly curled hair which in the barber shop fell away like black snow and was swept up like rabbit dung. Now Walter, his own son, called him down for being a hypocrite and not respecting his own Black woman.

"I have to talk you," he'd said. "I don't want Mama to hear us."

He'd returned to the car, opened it and, once Walter was in, they'd driven off, not speaking until they were on the parkway, driving east towards Long Island. He'd thought things hadn't gone well at Howard but he waited for his son to speak.

"I didn't want to believe it when I heard it, Papa," he'd said, his face turned arrogantly away.

"Heard what?"

"About your whore."

"My what?"

"Your white whore, Papa. Man, you can't hide things like that. Lionel McKinney and Horace Barnes came into the city last week and said they saw you with her. Holding hands, all lovey-dovey at a restaurant in the Village."

The rage which had built up after the argument with Elizabeth had passed and his son's words, rather than producing further complications, had at first served the purpose of relieving him of responsibility, of pretense, of serving as a model. It was as if all at once a great weight had been lifted from him, one which he had carried for too long. He'd wanted to laugh, but knew it would only anger Walter further and he would not be able to explain Elizabeth to him. But Walter hadn't wanted an explanation.

"And let me tell you something, Papa," he'd said. "I'm not concerned about you laying up there with whitey. Hell, no! What worries me is that somewhere along the line you didn't buy your own rap. Oh, listen, man. I went for it and that was enough, wasn't it? Black is beautiful and all that jive, right? As long as I went for it that was enough, wasn't it? As long as I went with it, you had no worries. Just like an old white massa, Papa? Ain't that the way it is?"

Lou'd never seen Water express his anger in that manner, shouting at the top of his voice while the two of them rode alone in the darkness, the highway nearly deserted. He thought of the relief he was now experiencing from his son's rage and compared it to the therapeutic effects of anger vented collectively in riots and civil disorder. But the feeling of relief had only lasted a few moments and then he gripped the steering wheel, wanting to veer off the road and crash into the trees.

"You bribed me, didn't you, Papa?" Walter had said. "Bribed me with all the Blackness and pride. Don't get me wrong. I'm grateful. You made me see how useless it is to get acceptance from the man other than on his terms. But I feel sorry for you. You couldn't pass for white and now you can't pass for Black."

Lou Torres hadn't spoken nor offered any words in his defense until they were back in front of the house. He said he was sorry. But the heaviness had returned and each porch light, each neatly manicured lawn and clipped hedge along the perfectly spaced row of homes seemed to mock his folly.

And the next day he returned to her, to that sweet white specter who haunted him, and he cried quietly, letting the ghost-like hands run over his body, soothing the tiredness of spirit which had engulfed him, recalling then his mother's white fingers on his forehead as she eased him into sleep after the Latin Saracens had jumped him in Central Park and had beaten him, then stolen his baseball glove. They had called him a nigger boy, while through his tears he'd tried to explain that he was one of them. The words, the magic words of street Spanish, of jive-Spanish, of please-man-don't-hit-me-anymore-spic-Spanish did not form on his *bemba*, his thick *negrito lindo* lips, his tongue tied in knots and the smell of urine drifting up to him as he crouched, not feeling the wetness but only the thin, almost aromatic smell. Oh, God, don't hit me again, please. When he arrived home, his mouth swollen and his eyes nearly closed, his father, in a black suit and tie and fear sculpted on his face, made him kneel and pray for those who had degraded him.

"They were Spanish, Papi," he'd said, tasting the raw places inside his mouth.

"It doesn't matter what they were, son," his father had said. "You must find it in your heart to forgive them."

"They couldn't tell I was Spanish, Papi."

"Yes, yes, Luis," his father repeated. "Pray now. We're all sons of our Lord Jehovah."

"They thought I was a *moreno*, Mami. Am I, Mami?"

And then praying, kneeling on the linoleum covered floor, his eyes closed and his insides paining him, the pain coming more from the realization that his own had injured him, rejected him, classified him with the faceless Black forms which each day surrounded his life, narrowed his world and attempted to erase his existence forever. Evelyn and Marissa and Jackie all watched him, their young eyes trying to understand what had happened. Only Ronald, fifteen and already gone his own way, gritted his teeth and later told him he was going to get a piece and go after the Saracens. The next month he caught Ronald coming up from the backyard with Bingo and Dusty, all three of them nodding and scratching, and when they were alone Ronald made him swear not to tell their parents.

Lying in the darkness, the soft lips caressing his chest, her breasts on him, soothing him to sleep as his mother had long ago, and from a deep and troubled sleep waking to hear his son's voice chastising him for his betrayal, the words had now imprinted on him as part of his conscience.

The shuttle bus arrived. A few students followed him on and moments later the bus was moving down the tree-lined road and onto the highway toward the town. Walter had eventually understood, but things were never the same between them, the power of their relationship having shifted into Walter's hands. After Elizabeth there had been others, their pale skin strangely attractive. Eventually his wife Charlene, haggard, aged beyond her years, had returned to Baton Rouge, knowing he was beyond help, giving up after Bonita went off to school.

At the train station, Lou Torres mechanically extracted his commuter pass, and when the train arrived, he boarded it. As the train moved in its rhythmic, sleep-inducing march to the city, Torres began to relax. He was safe once more, free of the pretense and endless attempts at brilliance. The house in Queens was up for sale. It would bring in plenty of money now that more Black middle class families were beginning to move into the area in greater numbers.

At Penn Station Torres hurried through the afternoon rush, entered the subway and headed for his high-rise Greenwich Village apartment. Once inside he mixed himself a drink, dialed the student's number, feeling for a moment that perhaps he had misunderstood the young woman's intent and she truly wanted his help. The voice on the other end made his body immediately alive with anticipation. He gave her the address and a half hour later she was there. Twenty years old, no more, the limp hair framing the wide, seemingly innocent eyes, her words weaving a spell over him so that at least for the moment he felt no regrets. She had transferred from Binghamton; literature major; parents divorced; always liked jazz rather than rock. Afterwards: as always, hearing in his own mind the words of contrast, the images which he could never get down on paper, his hand dormant on her breast, the fingers like strips of land on a map, a delta, night and day, shadow and light. Drifting off to sleep, he thought about Ronald at Greenhaven Prison. Lou Torres would be fifty-eight when Ronald came up for parole in ten years. Ronald would be sixty-one.

"Ama be all right, Lou," he'd said the last time Lou had visited him. "This time I ain't gonna mess around, man. How's Mami?"

"She's okay, Ron," he'd said. "Said she'd be up to see you Sunday."

"She did all right, didn't she? Four out of five ain't bad. A nurse, an artist, a lawyer and a college professor. That's a damn good percentage."

"Yeah, I guess it is," Lou answered, feigning sorrow.

"Walt's gonna be a doctor in a month or two, ain't he?"

"Six weeks."

"Ama tell you something, bro. You're lucky you never messed with the white lady. She's sweet but she sure can jack up a man."

And then the sleepiness was gone from his body and he was recalling every thing very quickly: his childhood, high school, the Army, Korea, Japan, college, Charlene, Walter, Bonita, Elizabeth and the ones that followed, his returning to New York with a graduate scholarship and a bride who turned heads, both black and white, his poetry in quarterlies, NYU and the others, the Superspics, and now all of them foundering, drowning, each in his own way lost in America forever. Dan Cartagena had told him his brother Ray had committed suicide on the West Coast. The tragedy of his friend's death had initially touched him but he had steeled himself to it. Ray Cartagena had been the best and the brightest of them and hadn't been able to make it all the way. The thought jolted him and he shook the girl awake.

"Get dressed," he said, roughly.

"Do you have to go somewhere?" she asked.

"My son's graduating tomorrow. I have to fly to Boston this afternoon. I'm sorry. Get dressed."

"I can help you get ready?" she said, shaken and hurt.

"I'll be okay. Hurry up."

His mind, his entire body was filled with new energy; each thought triggered a promise to himself, a dream to be fulfilled. The volume of poetry he had meant to compile, the historical novel about Charlene's family, the unfinished papers to submit had all taken on a new meaning. He was certain this time he'd get to them.

"Will I see you again?" the girl said once she was dressed and ready to go.

"Sure," he said. "I'll call you as soon as I get back. Okay, white lady?"

Torres slapped her buttocks and the girl laughed uncomfortably, not quite understanding his meaning. When she was gone he packed, showered, shaved and got dressed, feeling better than he had in weeks. A taxi to 42nd Street, a Carey bus and he was on the shuttle headed for Boston and then Cambridge to immense pride in Walter's accomplishment. Once airborne, he sat back and thought about Ronald in prison, his wasted life. He'd wanted to tell him that he was wrong, that it was three out of five, because he'd gone the same way, but he knew Ronald wouldn't have understood and the time for explanations and apologies and amending his life had passed. How many years had he left? His father had died at fifty-five. The autopsy said he had the body of a seventy year old man. Torres tried to think about the outline for the novel, but the girl's face, her body, the pale skin intruded into his thoughts and he gave up, feeling once again the stupor of the experience, knowing, shamelessly, that he'd call her as soon as he returned.

Sated for the moment, Lou Torres slept.

AN APOLOGY TO THE MOON FURIES

Last year, on one of those damp gray afternoons in late fall when remembrances of lost youth flail at the spirit like the broken-winged agony of a fallen bird, Dan Cartagena, standing under an umbrella, the sickly smell of flowers burning his nostrils and the soft rain mixing with his tears as they fell to the ground, watched friends and relatives move in the fog-like drizzle, each person shrouded in his own pain and, much as the shadows they were themselves destined to become, dutifully performed the empty rituals which helped him lay his brother Raymond to rest.

The chill opaque light struggling to find its way through the evergreens, the dark clothing of mourning, the tactful heaviness of the minister's words, the whispered regrets and averted looks seemed, rather than funereal, a somber if mocking celebration of the haunting sadness which had always clouded his brother's life.

As the expensive coffin was lowered into the earth, memories, like guests who've overstayed and materialize at inopportune times to break the established rhythm of a household, flitted in and out of Cartagena's consciousness. While flowers and clods of softened clay were tossed into the grave, he recollected events and tried matching them to family photographs. Primarily, however, his mind appeared obsessed with his brother's first painting, the sole reality which still held him as if in bondage to Raymond. The family photos, curled, yellowed by time, their images dated and out of place, lay in an old but remarkably well-preserved cigar box in the bottom right-hand drawer of his father's desk. Nearly six feet in length, the desk was a massive, intricately carved, nine drawer antique with pewter handles rather than knobs. The first genuine family heirloom, it was the seat of family power and the place from which his father had conducted business. Cartagena had inherited the desk and all its incumbent responsibilities seemingly years before his father's death.

In contrast to the desk, which he had accepted as a requisite yoke for his advancement, his brother's painting had always been a more significant symbol and one which he had never deciphered. Like a physical deformity which makes others uncomfortable, the painting hung in the living room of Cartagena's Manhattan apartment, clashing, his ex-wife had always insisted, with its decor. Still garishly brilliant in color, bordered the past twelve years by a gilded frame, it seemed alive and demanding of constant attention while transforming itself with time into a reminder of distance and loneliness but mostly of longing; each day rather than becoming an answer to his relationship to Raymond, folding back into itself like darkly violet dreamwaves to further complicate unanswered questions about him.

Complying with his mother's wishes to have Raymond buried next to his father in New York, Cartagena had flown to California for his body. Ilse had seemed relieved. Cartagena could never bring himself to call her Raymond's wife. In spite of his legal training, his mind rebelled against the common law equality. Similarly, the words "friend," "lady," and "woman" proved inadequate. One of those passive, kind, inoffensive women who manage to adapt themselves to their mate's needs, Ilse had been, in Cartagena's assessment, merely an attendant to Raymond's misery.

Austere, reserved, removing himself objectively from the aura of pathos surrounding the situation, Cartagena made no moral judgment about Ilse's apparent lack of grief and polite refusal to fly back to New York for the funeral. Granting the living the prerogative of amends, he rationalized her actions by telling himself that Ilse had been the one to personally endure his brother's pain the past ten years. His suicide, while not an easy matter for the family to accept, had been predictable, given his life prior to knowing her. The Beat Generation, peyote jello, Kerouac's credo, West Coast Jazz and early morning Venice Beach wine and pot parties. And yet her Scandinavian coldness, her almost Oriental resignation to his death, didn't sit well with him. Cartagena found himself needing to ask what had finally driven Raymond to his death. Sensing that any explanation she offered would only multiply his confusion, Cartagena held back and, as he had done as long as he could recall, carried out his responsibilities diplomatically, efficiently. Legal briefs, after all, were intended to state facts, not create drama. The touch of creativity emerged in compiling information, not in making it entertaining.

To avoid post-funeral chatter and inevitable family invitations to dinner and commiseration, Cartagena excused himself and sought out his cousin Peter. A member of the other Cartagenas, the ones his own family, excepting Raymond, had treated so distantly, Peter was a perfect listener. Educated, sophisticated, and seemingly content with his life, in spite of a broken marriage, Peter had developed into the only one of their generation who had managed to overcome the stigma of being an immigrant's child.

They got into Peter's car, rode slowly out of the cemetery and, once on the highway with Peter handling the Mercedes effortlessly, Cartagena began opening up. As if his heart could no longer carry the weight of worrying about Raymond, since he had left home over twenty years before, Cartagena confessed that he had never truly known Raymond. "I guess people thought we were close," he

said. Peter Cartagena listened. He did not comment or offer explanations for
the tragedy. Instead, he concentrated on the road, slick now from the steady
downpour.

Growing up, Cartagena's perception of his brother had always been distorted.
He was more like a father than a brother. Unhappily, he was one of those itinerant
fathers who drift in and out of a child's life to leave voids which can only be filled
by fantasy. Raymond was rarely home in those days. Being away contributed to
Cartagena's awe. When Raymond did show up, Cartagena listened religiously to
his every word and imitated his brashness and quick wit among his own friends.
Understandably, they laughed and told him he was trying to act grown up. When
Cartagena was with his brother, no matter how much he tried preventing it, he
appeared, even to himself, hypnotized by Raymond.

"I couldn't believe the things he did, Pete. Or for that matter what the hell
was going on with him. I couldn't even tell if he liked me half the time. All I
wanted was for him to pay attention to me. And he did but it was like there was
something which held his interest more. I suppose I was jealous. With other
people he'd go a little nuts, you know. It was confusing as hell. Even as a kid
I could tell something was wrong. It was like he was going out of his way to be
misunderstood. Whenever he got into it with family or friends he seemed to be
asking, in some crazy, complicated way, to be injured. It got so I started hating
normal conversations."

Social intrigue, however, held little interest for Cartagena back then. Every
waking moment not spent thinking about Raymond was consumed by his passion
for the Brooklyn Dodgers. Hoping they finished on top to play the hated Yankees,
he followed their every move by filling notebooks with photos, box scores, press
stories and ticket stubs of Ebbets Field games.

"Ironically, the year Ray went into the service I experienced enough hatred
for a lifetime. It was during the Korean War, I guess. Between the North Koreans,
the Chinese and the New York Giants, my world turned completely dark."

While in the service and later in college, Raymond's visits to the Cartagena
house (he never felt it was his house) became milestones of unhappiness for the
family. During those rare visits, daily activities came to a standstill. Letters went
unanswered; important telephone calls were ignored; television schedules were
scrambled to fit his taste; shopping dates carefully planned by Cartagena's sisters
were canceled; and meals, the one enterprise which punctuated the natural flow of
the day, invariably were delayed. The household, unusually calm in Raymond's
absence, became a confusing aggregation of seething tempers, threats and injured
feelings.

Initially everyone laughed about Raymond's effect on them. With each visit,
however, the situation worsened. Each time he came home on leave he left
deeper wounds in all of them. After the war it became apparent that no one
could talk to him for longer than a few minutes without coming away scarred. If
it wasn't his mother's idiosyncratic attention to housekeeping detail, it was his

father's energetic drive in his law practice, or his sisters' concern with fashion and popular music. His arguments varied only in content, never in intensity. But the worst times were those when, out of a sense of what Cartagena now surmised was Raymond's idea of personal responsibility, his brother introduced questions of a philosophical nature. Within ever narrowing frameworks of ideas, he challenged everyone with the expanding universe, the origins of the human species and the relationship between time and space, subjects which in spite of their apparent importance had no immediate relevance to people attempting to meet car payments, worrying over mortgages, advancing themselves at whatever they were doing, and above all forgetting the Marine Tiger, that real and oftentimes metaphorical ship which brought thousands of their people to New York.

Raymond's attacks on his father, it had seemed to Cartagena as he listened to the minister offer a prayer for his brother's soul earlier, had been the most unjustified of all. The four of them— Raymond, Angie, Fran and he himself— had been the recipients of his father's hard work and relative financial success, a reality preferable to Raymond's world of unformed ideas and painful experiences. It was a world, as much as Raymond may have disliked its plastic and somewhat shallow aspects, which provided the family with a spacious two story house in Rockaway, music lessons (and ballet for Angie and Fran), summers away from the city and an almost paradisiac existence, compared to what they heard about or read in newspapers concerning other Puerto Rican families.

As if time possessed a quality not measured in minutes, Raymond would spend hours, sometimes days, belaboring a point. Like a skilled boxer, he dodged, jabbed and hooked words into others, waiting patiently for signs of fatigue, injury or loss of concentration. Without mercy, unconscious of his emotional killer instinct, he'd deliver his knockout punch: a line from an obscure play, the name of an equally obscure Dutch painter, the lowest ERA of a pitcher with a last place club, or the migratory habits of the Canadian goose. It didn't matter. Engaging all comers in a fierce battle over the most insignificant of points, and with only the slightest provocation, Raymond expounded on politics, music, books, science, religion and any other subject anyone had the audacity to mention in passing while he was present.

During these exhibitions of mental agility, Cartagena stood very still and watched Raymond wave his long arms, frowning one minute, laughing sarcastically the next, driven, Cartagena imagined in later years, by intellectual demons. Possessed, his brother would pace the floor pleading his case as if it were of supreme importance that things were seen his way. More often than not, people gave up and granted him the point, leaving him to grow dark and morose once more.

"I mean, watching Raymond operate was like watching the Dodgers play. The score never told you what the other team had gone through, the humiliation. He would have been a great lawyer. That's what the old man used to say, anyhow."

And yet, like the Dodgers of the fifties, thought Cartagena as his cousin turned the car into the Long Island Expressway, there was something tragic and quite frail about Raymond Cartagena, almost as if he were too good to be true and whatever held him together was quite tenuous.

"There was a difference of seven years between us, Pete. It seemed like twenty-seven, he was so far out sometimes. I was never one of his targets and to this day I can't figure out why. I guess it was my awe of the guy. He was like a magician. I couldn't wait for him to come home. You can't imagine what it was like living out there. Never mind that we were the only P.R.'s for miles around. Everything became boring very quickly. I used to think Rockaway was the place where fads came to die. All the kids were crazy about the Dodgers. We all collected baseball cards and whenever we weren't involved in flipping them or trading them, we'd sit around talking about how much we hated girls and how dumb our teachers were."

Raymond's seemingly tough manner and his vast knowledge easily made him the most complex person Cartagena knew at the time. And yet in spite of the burden he'd had to carry the past twenty years, he could recall the kindness which always came through. Of all the memories, these were the most difficult to accept. When Raymond was away, Cartagena spent long hours recalling his visits, wishing for his return so that in the spur of the moment, oblivious of time or schedules, he'd ask Cartagena if he wanted to go for a walk and they'd end up in the Bronx Zoo after riding the subway for nearly two hours. Or he'd take him to visit his friends, all of whom were strange and exotic in their long beards and sandals even in winter, their women so pale and spacy and sweet. Or they'd just walk, and speaking very softly he'd tell him, in precise detail, of the places he'd visited, how the people dressed, what they ate and what language they spoke.

There was always a sadness to his voice then. A sadness produced by not being able to recapture all he had experienced in his travels. Unlike most people who accept this fact as one of the failings of being human, Raymond Cartagena fought against it, punishing himself because he couldn't recall the exact colors of the boat which carried him from Pireefs to Mikonos; he was not content with his description of the chalk-white chapels etched, almost carved, against the metallic blue sky, the brilliant sunlight ringing the whiteness so that even Cartagena as a child heard the color.

Softly, always softly, he talked about greens and blues when he told about the waters of the Aegean, so that his words compelled Cartagena to look below the shimmering surface of the sea and in his mind's eye capture each stone and sea urchin. And then, Raymond, wracking his poor tortured soul, would begin to grow dark and angry because he couldn't recall the colors of the boat and couldn't lie about it.

"Even then he didn't turn against me, Pete. Can you understand that? It was like he was protecting me. The thing would only last a few seconds with me and then he was back to himself and talking quietly again. I mean I really believe the other stuff was a front. You know, defenses."

He was a great storyteller and without much effort Cartagena was transported to far-off places, Raymond's mesmerizing voice weaving incredible tales set in bazaars in North Africa, his language fluid and rich, filled with foreign words which Cartagena was certain were being pronounced exactly as they were meant to be, this later proven by listening to him speak a dozen languages fluently. When Raymond spoke Cartagena was there. Rabat, Sidi Slimane, Casablanca, Tripoli—all of them Air Force bases from which Raymond explored the world— *minaret, caliph, bedouin*; painting camel caravans miles long as they made their way ribbon-like across a desert sunset, the sound of the words lingering so that there were tones between them. "That was a *muezzin* calling the faithful to worship from the *minaret*," he'd say and Cartagena was spellbound by the whining sounds; and he'd tell of drums and belly dancers so that alone at night Cartagena still found himself at the age of thirty-eight haunted by the sensuous flesh of a dancer, her feet bare and her finger cymbals never fading until he fell asleep, stopping at times to gaze into the distance of his mind as if on the shore of an immense river deep in the Amazon jungle, pausing to reflect on some inner sorrow before continuing his painful journey, whisking him away, this time to a landing on the South Pole during a snowstorm, stressing, so that Cartagena never forgot, that only on that pole, not on its opposite, were penguins to be found.

"He tried to teach me Morse Code a couple of times. That's what he did on the plane. He was a radio operator. I never caught on but it never bothered him. I guess he knew I enjoyed his company. I'm willing to bet he enjoyed playing big brother to me and that was all there was to it. But God help me, Pete. I feel used by him. The times I saw him as an adult he was always kind and encouraging but it was like he knew something about me that I'd never be able to understand. I don't know. Maybe I'm just angry at the waste."

Raymond spent four years in the Air Force, was discharged and returned home for a couple of months before leaving again for California to attend college on the G.I. Bill, refusing his father's offer of financial help. One evening when Raymond had been home barely a week, there was a violent argument between him and his father over Raymond's statement that he'd never get married because he disliked children, adding that women were only good for one thing and it wasn't for having children. Cartagena hadn't understood Raymond's side of the argument but never asked anyone about it, fearing that a discovery of his ignorance would destroy their alliance. Cartagena had been deeply wounded by the remark, however. For weeks, feeling betrayed, he avoided Raymond. Eventually Raymond became aware of the silence and, without asking him what had caused the withdrawal, told him that it hadn't been his intention to hurt his feelings. "I guess I was thinking of myself as a kid," he'd said. "I wasn't very good at it, Danny," he'd added, smiling sadly, awkwardly. "I stunk at everything. Sports, school, girls, friendship. Everything seemed senseless. The only thing I could do well was remember stuff nobody else did."

His father had been quite angry, a rarity for him. He ended up telling

Raymond that being logical was good only up to a point. Raymond made a gesture of disgust and, muttering something about ignorance and stupidity, walked out of his father's study. Head down, Raymond came upstairs to draw. Although he generally spent his time sketching nature, whenever any unpleasantness took place between him and his father, Raymond attempted to draw people. As if whatever was hurting him were literally spilling out through his fingers and onto his drawing pad, he created ugly people, whose faces, disfigured by pain, their bodies twisted grotesquely and their hands gnarled, struggled to free themselves from the paper.

They were similar to Goya's sketches of war, except that they had a quality of their own. The eyes of the people were especially tragic. In Goya one saw the horror in people's eyes, but in Raymond's sketches there was more. In his drawings the horror was obvious but beyond it there was a profound awareness, a self-consciousness, a watching of their own humanity crumbling before them without their being able to check the process.

Four months before Raymond swallowed a bottle of pills and was found dying at the bottom of a cliff below his house in Big Sur, *The Western Review of the Arts* called him one of the most promising artists of the decade. This was after a number of successful shows in the San Francisco area. His paintings were selling well and little seemed to be standing in his way. And yet it hadn't been enough to sustain him. Ilse's letters to Angie, with whom she had established an odd bond, considering the difference in the two women, were always filled with melancholic apology: "Yesterday we had friends over for rum punch and fruit cake. We decorated the Christmas tree and watched the sun set. A warm breeze was blowing from the south and Ray said it smelled like snow. Lorne told him his nose was drunk because the radio said it was sixty-seven degrees. Ray went up into his studio and stayed there the rest of the evening." It was as if she were responsible for Raymond's unhappiness, a trait Cartagena often thought she must have acquired from him, who, as his life drew to a close, spent more and more of his time absorbing everyone else's pain. The assassinations, the farmworkers, the Soledad Brothers, war resisters and the Vietnam War had all taken their toll on his brother.

At the funeral his mother cried and told Angie that Raymond should've married Ilse. "What's going to become of her and the children?" she asked no one, lost and alone in her sorrow, recalling perhaps the time Lorne and Melissa had spent with her two years before. Ilse and Raymond had gone off to Rhodes for six months and when they returned the twins were chattering away in Greek, as if born to it. Their transformation had pleased Raymond, but within a week he was into one of his dark moods, ranting and raving about the Greek dictatorship. Towards the end he no longer argued with anyone but would sit for hours, pensive, troubled, the area around him laden with tension.

Raymond, guessed Cartagena, was a genius who had somehow become aware that it wasn't enough to be able to see. He seemed driven by a need to prove himself far greater than anyone he'd known. No one, as far as he knew, least of all Cartagena himself, had ever been able to figure out the standards by which Raymond measured himself. Cartagena was certain, however, that whenever his brother approached the perfection he sought, he found flaws in himself undetectable by anyone else.

Gifted as Raymond proved to be, his father was not far behind. He was a hard worker and, unlike Raymond, had no need for self-scrutiny, limiting his power of discernment to his legal practice. A master of the compromise, he never lost his temper beyond the point where a situation could not be immediately repaired. Although he never talked about himself or his background to his children, their mother filled in the details of his life, creating for them a hero, whom Raymond, Cartagena often imagined, could never surpass or, worse yet, equal.

"Papa ran away from home at the age of sixteen," his mother had once said to them. "There were nine other children in the family. They worked at picking coffee and tobacco in the hills around Cacimar, in the center of the island. Even though we were both from the area, my family never knew any of his relatives until we got married. My family lived in the town and his lived in the country. He was a country boy. A *jíbaro*. Very smart and very serious, but very suspicious, like all of his people. And always polite. Anyway, he left home, made his way to the capital and worked around the docks. When he had enough money, he paid his way on board a ship bound for New York. That was around 1929 or '30 and things weren't too good anywhere."

His mother's eyes had become misted with remembering and she had then told them about Juan Cartagena working in a factory, studying English and going to school at night. Eventually, he graduated from City College. In his junior year, working as an accountant for the factory which had originally hired him, he met and married Teresa Beltrán. Driven, Cartagena often imagined, much like Raymond but in a more conventional way, his father continued to work as an accountant and began law school. Six years later he finished his law studies and passed the bar examination. Raymond was already eight when his father opened his first office in downtown Brooklyn. In the family photo album there was still a picture of Juan Cartagena in cap and gown, his wife and two of his children, Raymond and Angela, in front of them. Ray is wearing a double-breasted suit and a wide tie. Frances had been three or four at the time and too young to take to the graduation. Cartagena himself had arrived, almost as an afterthought he had often been told, the previous year.

Gifted with a remarkable memory, it was conceivable that Raymond had stored every injury ever received during those years, each emotional setback, each minor disappointment, adding to his misery and confusion about himself.

As his cousin slowed down to enter the Grand Central Parkway, now bumper to bumper and moving carefully because of the driving rain, Cartagena recalled how once in a while Raymond would talk to him about living in a walkup apartment in El Barrio, to this day a foreign country to him. When he talked about those days, his voice became almost inaudible, his manner totally subdued.

"One time he took me to the building where he had lived with my parents, Pete. I guess it was his first recollection of a home."

The neighborhood was like nothing Cartagena had ever seen. He had been frightened by the harshness of the people, the squalor, the garbage in the empty lots and the incredible summer din of the street. The colors, the smells and sounds seemed strangely forbidden. Like invisible ocean waves they attacked his senses relentlessly. Cartagena had shaken his head violently when Raymond had pulled him over to a store in whose window there rested shining and wrinkled pig ears, tails, snouts and what Raymond later explained were pig's intestines filled with a mixture of rice, spices and pig's blood. Cartagena's eyes had behaved as if they had a will of their own when confronted with the dazzling carnage of what had once been an animal. His eyes darted from the woman's thick, greasy fingers to the black-brown sausage. But Raymond had been very gentle and spoke about being a little boy. Carefully, Cartagena chose a codfish fritter, a *bacalaíto*, bit gingerly into the crisp batter and liked it.

The black woman had appeared to recognize Raymond. They had spoken in Spanish for a few minutes but Cartagena hadn't understood their coded language. Years later, when friends talked about people talking Puerto Rican, Cartagena had been angry. He insisted and as best as he could tried to explain that Puerto Ricans spoke Spanish. Privately, however, he had to admit that although the language was Spanish, it was ciphered and sifted through the common experience of harried people to protect themselves from outsiders, the language twisting and turning uncomfortably, the words five, six, seven times removed from their original meaning, so that when they were spoken one could tell immediately whether the person was friend or foe; never knowing whether one's very own presented a threat except through the language.

Raymond had then asked him if he'd like to go for a boat ride and they'd walked west to the park. After he'd paid for the boat rental and they were walking towards the edge of the lake, he'd spoken about how he and his father and mother would come to Central Park and rent a boat every Sunday afternoon in the summertime. "I cried when we moved away," he'd said once they were in the boat and he'd begun rowing. "It was safer then. I don't mean it was really safe, because there were fights and fires, but I felt safe. The same thing in Brooklyn. We'd go to Prospect Park or to Coney Island and walking home in late afternoon I'd feel tired but good. When we got the house I was glad at first but then I don't know what happened. I didn't miss the apartment in Brooklyn but kept thinking about the one here in El Barrio. I missed walking up the five flights after school. There was an old man who flew pigeons from the roof. Don Zoilo. He had hundreds of them and he'd let me feed them. You would've liked it here, Danny."

And then he said something which Cartagena only lately began to understand and which haunted him almost as much as what took place before Raymond left for California the first time. They were out in the middle of the lake when Raymond suddenly stopped rowing. For a few minutes the boat drifted lazily in the afternoon breeze and Cartagena could feel the sun on his arms. "We grow up too fast, Danny. All of us. We leave our memories behind. Mama and Papa in P.R. and me here, in some dark hall or alley, some backyard full of broken glass and junk. I don't remember where I left mine, so I keep coming back." Cartagena had watched Raymond's long delicate hand trail in the water, the fingers rippling the surface ever so slightly. "I guess it can't be helped," he'd said. "We leave them behind like old shoes, Danny. We get caught up in getting ahead and we forget our memories and where we came from. And then we hurt and we don't know why."

The night of the argument with his father, his mother came into Raymond's room to say goodnight and asked him why he argued so much. Thrown off balance by her concern, Raymond shrugged his shoulders like a little boy. Confronted directly, he was reduced to his simplest self. But his explanations then hardly went beyond a shrug. This time, mustering up a defense, he quickly explained that he enjoyed arguing. "I don't believe in anything, Mama," he'd said, proudly. "I can take either side and do all right. I guess I'm lucky."

Cartagena didn't understand much of what Raymond argued about. He recalled asking his sisters on numerous occasions about the nature of the disputes. The only information ever provided by them came in the form of warnings, stressing above all that the wisest course was to stay away from Raymond, at all costs never repeat any of his crazy ideas, and always believe in God.

It was apparent to Cartagena even then that his sisters lived in mortal fear of Raymond's words. Although strong spirited girls possessing their brother's stubborn streak, they individually lacked his stamina. Only when they joined forces and employed some exotic feminine ruse, such as crying and exaggerating their emotional injury, did they succeed in stalemating him. Generally, they steered clear of him. If he happened to come into a room and found them talking, they immediately busied themselves with dusting figurines, straightening picture frames, or closing or opening drapes.

He always knew what they were up to and laughed at them. The day after the argument with his father, Raymond surprised Angie and Fran in the dining room while they were setting the table for supper. They were talking about Angie's engagement to Kevin Monahan. She and Kevin had met at Brooklyn College and, even though Angie was just in her first year, they had decided to get married. Raymond told them that marriage wasn't for getting a new house and clothes and a car like they did in the movies. He told them that it was all they ever thought about and didn't they have anything inside their heads other than pictures from magazines showing the perfect American housewife in her perfect American home. Angie told him that she didn't know what he was talking about, since he wasn't ever going to get married, so that it wasn't any of his business what they talked about.

Momentarily stymied, Raymond recuperated and informed them that precisely because he saw what empty-headed things women were, he had decided not to get married. It wasn't much of a retort but the forcefulness of his voice was enough to quiet them. After the four years Raymond was away, his sisters grew to tolerate him, much in the same fashion as his mother. Rather than caving in and becoming emotional as they had done in the past, they now indulged his every whim without paying much attention to his words. Although still rattled, they were able to maintain some semblance of composure. "We're not that bad, are we, Ray? Well ... Maybe you're right," Angie'd said. "Have you had anything to eat? Supper's almost done, if you'd like to sit down. We're having spaghetti."

Their attitude angered Raymond and, disregarding their newly found sophistication concerning the management of the unruly male of the species, he battered relentlessly at their defenses. Within ten minutes he had once again reduced them to hysteria and the only thing which saved him from physical attack was the fact Angie and Fran had developed into beautiful young women and spent a great deal of time out of the house at the school and on picnics, dates, shopping trips into Manhattan, which like everyone else around them, they called The City. Their schedule did not allow for protracted battles. On that day, they were due at a baby shower for one of Angie's girlfriends. This time, however, unable to withstand another minute of Raymond's sarcasm, they rose against him and, screaming, forced him to retreat up the stairs, laughing as he went. "You're nuts, Ray!" screamed Angie, going four or five steps after him. "Nuts! That's what you are." Fran, not daring to go any higher than the bottom step, added that Raymond should be locked up and the key thrown away. No one thought much about the incident.

Something, however, had happened to Raymond in the exchange. For the next twenty-four hours he remained in his room. He emerged then, unshaven, his lanky body stooped over and his hair nest-like. As if attempting to blind himself, he kept pressing his eyes into his head. When his mother asked him what was the matter, he told her he'd been working on a painting. He began rummaging through the refrigerator and piling bread, cheese, ham, pickles, the mustard jar and a pitcher of orange juice on a big platter, he returned to his room. When he came down the next morning he looked worse than before.

"He smelled so badly that Mom told him to go upstairs and take a bath, Pete. Without a word, he nodded, told her she was right and like a little kid went up, took a bath and went to sleep for the next thirty-six hours."

The next time the Cartagena family saw Raymond he was dressed in penny loafers, a pair of gray slacks, a buttoned-down shirt with an Ivy League tie and one of the Harris Tweed jackets he'd purchased in Scotland while on a stopover. He had shaved, combed his hair and looked like every mother's dream. It was Sunday morning and Raymond accompanied the family to church. Juan Cartagena, seizing opportunity where he found it, although not a man given to religious sentiment, had joined the Lutheran Church. The move had allowed him to retain some of the trappings of the Catholic faith of his youth and incorporate the Protestantism of the country which had so readily adopted him. The pastor, Dr. Ewing, was so shocked to see Raymond that he spent a full ten minutes in a rather convoluted digression from his sermon and spoke about the "prodigal son," a concept which Cartagena had not yet understood nor cared to.

"I thought it meant insane," said Cartagena as his cousin approached the Triborough Bridge. "Really, in my mind the word had distinct connotations of mental imbalance. I suppose the inference back then was that Ray was wasting his life."

When the family returned home from church, everyone seemed relaxed and in a pleasant mood. Angie and Fran had chosen to forget about their run-in with Raymond and were back to being solicitous and charming. This lasted for the better part of the afternoon and evening. After supper Raymond informed the family that he had a surprise. With a naiveté which far exceeded her contrived lack of intelligence, Angie asked if it was something which he had brought back from Morocco and had not yet shown them. "No, nothing like that," Raymond had said, smiling in his strange way so that his sisters didn't know whether he was being friendly or mocking them. "It's a portrait of the two of you." Angie then asked if that's what he had been doing up in his room all that time. Raymond nodded sheepishly and Fran turned to their mother and said, "Isn't that sweet, Mama?"

Their mother nodded politely and looked at her husband, who, it seemed to Cartagena, had known all along what Raymond was up to. With this, Raymond went bounding up the stairs. When he returned he was carrying his easel. There appeared to be a painting on the easel but he had draped a sheet over them both. He set the easel down in the middle of the living room and with great theatrical gestures, removed the sheet to reveal his first actual oil painting.

"It was fantastic, Pete. I mean both ways. Really great and totally far out. I mean, you've seen it."

In the foreground of the large canvas a young man was racing headlong, the lines of motion of his naked body so beautifully outlined, so perfect, his flight so desperate that it appeared as if in the next second he would plunge out of the painting and into their midst. As in Raymond's ink drawings, the face was etched with indescribable agony, the fear in the young man's eyes calling out desperately. He was being pursued by two women dressed in evening gowns, one white, the other yellow. The faces of the two women were television screens, each with a miniature painting on them. With their arms outstretched they seemed about to dig their talon-like scarlet fingernails into the young man's back. In the background, across a desolate violet and blue horizon, twelve moons delicately hued in golden light drifted over desert mountains.

The more Cartagena stared at the painting, the more convinced he became that something terrible was about to happen. No one spoke and the eerie light of the painting, the yellow moons, the long, blood-filled claws seemed to glow.

Way out, beyond the consciousness of the moment, Cartagena heard the water pounding the beach, the sound growing solidly until it became a steady hum inside of him. His father was the first to speak but he didn't understand him. It had seemed more as if their father were uttering a prayer. For years Cartagena regretted his intrusion into the silence to praise his brother's creation, believing the praise should have come from someone else. "It looks like what you told me about the Sahara," he'd said.

Raymond had smiled and nodded his approval. Angie and Fran said not a word. They remained in their seats, glancing at the painting and then at each other and at their mother for what seemed too long. The spell was finally broken when the phone rang. Fran jumped up and announced it was for her. She raced out of the living room and upstairs. With perhaps a bit more decorum but with the same intent, Angie followed her. Raymond continued to smile until his father shook his head despairingly and Raymond draped the sheet over the painting. "I knew everyone would like it," he'd said, and hoisting the easel over his head, marched upstairs.

By this time his mother and sisters were convinced that Raymond had gone off the deep end. He became more argumentative and very slowly household activities began once more to revolve around his erratic behavior and schedule. He would come and go at all hours of the night and on more than one occasion brought home objects which inspired the family to believe that somewhere along the line they had mistreated Raymond and he was now paying them back. One evening, after informing them that he was going out in search of the truth, he returned with an enormous piece of driftwood, bleached almost white from exposure to salt and sun and polished smooth by the sand. It was nearly ten o'clock at night, but he managed to hold everyone's attention until midnight. He pointed out faces, shapes of countries, letters which formed words, which in turn, after involved logical sequences, spelled out messages. There were animals disguised as flowers and flowers disguised as jewels and on and on until everyone drifted away from him, making excuses as they left. That night Angie had a nightmare.

It was shortly after this that his mother decided that Raymond's trouble was lack of female companionship. In spite of his opposition, they arranged for him to meet Annie Pardo. Annie was Miguel Pardo's daughter. Don Miguel, was one of Juan Cartagena's clients. He owned an import-export company specializing in tropical foods, a moving company, twenty-five buildings in East Harlem and the South Bronx, several houses along Rockaway Beach and part interest in a hotel in Miami Beach.

Raymond, when he wanted to, had impeccable manners and a charm so delicate that he could disarm most women with his helplessness. For more than a week after he found out that Annie was coming to dinner, he behaved with infinite restraint in everything he did. Each word had the kind of caring and affection which amazed even his sisters. That Sunday he again went to church with the family.

Dressed and well scrubbed, he listened attentively to Dr. Ewing's sermon, something which on previous occasions he had been unable to do, choosing instead to keep up a whispered and sarcastic commentary on everything uttered by the silver haired minister.

Around four that afternoon, a limousine delivered Annie Pardo from Jamaica Estates and, after some preliminary chit-chat during which Raymond easily won Annie over and relieved Angie's last remnants of anxiety over his possible behavior, the family sat down to dinner.

Cartagena hadn't liked Annie Pardo then or now and his view of what took place had always been colored by his antipathy. She hadn't changed much in twenty-five years, so that at the time, she could best be described as she was today, a snob. In her second year at Barnard College, wealthy, quite beautiful, Annie Pardo was the Puerto Rican's answer to the Jewish American Princess, a PRAP. She had blonde hair and blue eyes, two genetic traits which impressed even Cartagena's parents, who as far as he could recall had never suffered from undue emphasis upon physical characteristics as a requisite for acceptance, the two of them being quite attractive in their own right and having produced in their olive-skinned, black hair offspring, four equally attractive specimens.

The incident with Annie Pardo began quite innocently with a discussion of art, a subject which, on a superficial level, she had apparently mastered. The family had gone through the meal, enjoying Doña Teresa's fine cooking: an enormous roast beef, mashed potatoes, peas and carrots and salad. She had just brought two freshly baked apple pies to the table and was on her way back to the kitchen for the ice cream when Raymond slapped his forehead in disbelief.

"What? What did you say?" he suddenly said to Annie.

During a spirited discussion on fashions, Annie had recounted her experiences in Europe the previous summer, extrapolating trends in dress to the subject of art and painting, in particular, coming to rest, more out of lack of breath than any derived conclusion, at her stay in Rome. Up to that point Raymond hadn't said much. When he didn't get the required response to his question, he informed Annie that Rome was a decadent city and that it hadn't produced any decent art in hundreds of years. In the light from the candles along the middle of the table, Raymond resembled a tiger, the feral tone of his voice making what he said more powerful than its content.

"Have you been there?" asked Annie, smiling, her head tilted coyly to one side and her eyes ready to tear into Raymond.

"Yes, several times," he replied, his gaze boring into Annie's. There was at those moments a quality to his voice which warned others not to trespass into his domain. Some, unschooled in this phenomenon of animal dynamics, went ahead and argued only to find themselves ridiculed by Raymond's counter-arguments. Annie, exposed to some measure of good breeding and waspish cattiness among her schoolmates, began backing off, seeking refuge in the safest possible area, common experience, hoping, Cartagena had imagined later, that Raymond, thus far behaving like a gentleman, would see that she recognized her blunder and spare her.

"Then you must have visited the Sistine Chapel," she said, brightly. "How did you like Michelangelo's work?" She had pronounced the name in Italian. Years later Cartagena understood her fascination for the Italian language and culture, since it became clear that she viewed herself as descended from Northern Italian nobility.

"Michelangelo was a tool of the state, a puppet of the ruling class and the Pope," shot back Raymond, angrily.

He could have said anything, because Annie's reaction was instantaneous. She blushed bright red, coughed twice into the back of her hand and answered him. "Are you an authority on Italian art?" she asked haughtily, her chin raised defiantly and her eyes attempting to pierce his.

"No, I'm not," Raymond said, calmly. "I am an artist." Annie laughed.

It was by no means derisive laughter but it might as well have been. Cartagena's suspicion had always been that she was shocked. Even after having Angie and Fran mention Raymond's drawing, she never imagined he would be as bold as to declare himself an artist. The scene became almost comical after that.

"You?" Annie'd sputtered, unable to contain her laughter.

"Yes, me," Raymond had said, pounding the table so that his dessert plate rose several inches and clattered noisily against Annie's glass. "I am an artist and you, blondie, are a phony. A little spic phony mascarading as an upper-class debutante, when all you are is a petit-bourgeois nitwit."

Cartagena recalled laughing at the entire thing until his brother said "petit bourgeois." He was suddenly convinced that Raymond had directed an ancient curse, learned from a Berber tribe, at Annie Pardo and that within seconds she would turn into a camel and begin braying. His father put a hand on Cartagena's arm and he immediately understood the gravity of the situation.

Annie Pardo was gasping for air and trying to get up from the table. Angie, Fran and their mother immediately went to her and escorted her upstairs to the bathroom. Once there she angrily disposed of her dinner, was washed and taken to Fran's room where she proceeded to faint. Raymond got up from the table, put on his coat and left the house. He was gone four days.

"When he came back he looked awful, Pete. His eyes were red from smoking grass and drinking and he hadn't shaved. I guess that's when he started growing a beard. He told me he'd stayed at his friend Albert's house in the Village. He looked just like one of his drawings."

Cartagena had just come in from school and Raymond smiled as if to tell him he was sorry. When he came downstairs that night, Raymond was clean shaven and looked better, but the worry lines on his forehead were etched deeper and he couldn't look his father in the eye. He offered no explanation for his behavior towards Annie Pardo and none was elicited from him. Angie and Fran lowered their heads when they saw him. His mother, looking extremely troubled, remained, as was her manner, impassive in the face of a crisis. Cartagena's father had had enough of his son's theatrics and remained in his study, refusing to join the family at supper.

Two days later at the supper table, Raymond announced that he was leaving for California to attend school. The announcement threw everyone into a panic. Angie was engaged to be married and the entire family, bound by tradition, had assumed, perhaps with some trepidation, that Raymond would remain in New York until June and serve as an usher or at least attend the ceremony and reception.

Another terrible argument ensued and Raymond informed the family that he had far more important things to do than attend a wedding, especially in a church. Cartagena's father told him that it was a shame that he did not feel enough love for his sister to remain home a few more months.

"Maybe that's why I'm leaving," Raymond had said, and turned away to go upstairs.

"Wait a minute," said his father.

"No, Dad," he said, turning. "I've waited long enough." His father watched him go upstairs and stood looking sadly after him. Cartagena guessed that Raymond meant to say that he loved Angie but it didn't seem that way. As the years passed and Angie's marriage ended in divorce, leaving her with two children to support, one of whom, Jamie, had to have periodic treatment on a kidney machine, Raymond's love for her became more apparent as he contributed to the medical expenses. But before he left for California, it all seemed complicated and strange. The very next day Raymond went out to say goodbye to his friends. He came back to the house and began packing, taking very few clothes but making sure he took all of his art books and paints. He strapped the easel to the largest of his suitcases and placed them in the hall outside his room.

That afternoon, before supper, Raymond asked him if Cartagena wanted to go for a walk. He was torn by the invitation, wishing to spend time with Raymond but not wanting it to be for the purposes of saying goodbye.

"How about it, Danny," he said, tousling his hair.

"Sure," Cartagena replied and shrugged his shoulders as if it didn't matter one way or the other. A big, lumpy dry feeling took over his throat and his chest became tight. "I guess I don't mind. Let me get my jacket."

He ran upstairs and before he got to his room he felt the tears. In the bathroom he pounded his head to make the tears stop and then splashed cold water on his face. When he was sure he wouldn't start crying again, he put on his jacket and ran back down. He had made up his mind to ask Raymond to take him along.

"Mama, Ray and I are going out for a walk," he said loudly as he reached the bottom of the stairs. He needed, if only for a brief moment, to cement the bond between him and Raymond, perhaps threatening with his words his own independence and instigating, if not worry, disquietude, that like Raymond he too would drift out of their lives and return transformed.

Outside, the sun had begun setting and the street lights were already lit along the row of neat, manicured lawns. The air was crisp and clear and a faint fragrance of salt water and flowers drifted in the spring breezes. They walked quietly down to the beach and then to the edge of the water to watch the horizon and the lights where the beach turned out to the point.

"Do you know why I have to go away?" Raymond asked after a while.

"No," Cartagena replied. "I guess you don't want Angie to marry Kevin."

Shrugging his shoulders, Raymond began walking parallel to the water.

"I don't care if she marries him," he'd said. "He's a nice guy. I just think she's going to be unhappy as hell in a few years. She's not a stupid woman, you know."

Cartagena wanted to tell him that Angie was not a woman, that she was their sister, a girl. He followed Raymond as he went on talking very softly and sadly with the sun going down and night beginning to cover them, the lights out on the point like stars millions of years into time.

"I love Angie and Fran and you and Mom and Dad, but I don't know how to show it the right way. Not like everyone else, anyway. I can't even say it too well because then I'd have to do certain things and if I didn't, I'd feel like a hypocrite. You know, like I was lying."

Cartagena hadn't quite understood what Raymond was talking about, but he knew that something terrible was eating away at his brother and that Raymond was sorry to be leaving. After a while Raymond was quiet and they just walked and walked until they were almost to the point. On their way back Raymond seemed to be feeling better. Cartagena asked him if he would write from California and Raymond said he would, if Cartagena wrote about everything he did in his baseball games. Cartagena said he would and then Raymond stopped, turned to watch the water and sat down on the sand. Cartagena sat next to him. Raymond then lay back and stretched his arms and legs so that he looked like a giant gingerbread man.

"Did you really like my painting?" he said, sounding to Cartagena like his friend, Joey Goldstein, who was always worried that people didn't like the things he wore, or what he said, or his birthday parties.

"Sure," Cartagena answered. "It was just like you told me about the Sahara. You know, blue and gold and the moon shining down on the pyramids, except you didn't have any pyramids. The women were horrible, though. I mean, you drew them good but they were. . .you know, scary. Were they supposed to be Angie and Fran?"

"Cut it out," he'd said, laughing. "That was a joke."

"Yeah, some joke."

"What do you mean?"

Raymond had been genuinely surprised.

"I think it scared them."

"Well, yeah. Some jokes are like that," Raymond had said, somberly. "I guess that's why I have to go. Everybody's too grown up around here."

"Like Angie and Fran?"

"Sure, like them. But it's everybody else. I don't mean you. You'll always be a kid like me. Everybody's got a little kid and a grown up inside of them. Everybody. One day the grown up joins the crowd and starts telling the kid to shut up so he can take over and run the show. I guess that's why I said I didn't want to have kids that time. I don't want to be the one to help them shut up. I can't even tell the kid inside of me to shut up. You know, tell him to behave. I guess I never will. But you liked it, huh?"

"I really did, Ray," Cartagena said, and then almost choked with emotion, because Raymond asked him if he wanted it.

"To keep?" he'd asked.

"Of course, to keep. I'll frame it for you."

"Really?"

"Yeah, sure," Raymond said, and turned over on the sand and began to wrestle with his brother. Cartagena laughed and laughed until his face hurt. When they stopped laughing and were lying exhausted on the sand, Cartagena asked his brother if he could go to California with him. Raymond didn't answer him, and when Cartagena asked him again, he shook his head.

"It wouldn't work out, Danny," he'd said. "You have to go to school and with me around, that would never happen. Even if you were older, it wouldn't work out. I have to do this alone. It's like when you're playing ball. Nobody can bat for you. You know that."

Raymond helped him up and they walked back to the house. His mother made them hot chocolate and said nothing about sand on the carpets. Raymond spent the rest of the evening making a frame for the painting. After framing the painting, he signed it down on the right-hand corner, his script hand so neat that it looked as if the name, Cartagena, had been stamped on.

"It's called 'An Apology to the Moon Furies'," he said when he was finished and was cleaning the thin, needle-like brush. "Will you remember? It doesn't mean anything. Just a joke between one kid and another."

Cartagena said he would remember, and Raymond nodded several times, his eyes sad as in his drawings, veiled and moist as if it were his turn to cry. He turned to the wall and hung the painting, taking an unusually long time to line it up. He then sat on Cartagena's bed, looked as if he was about to say something, got up and went to his own room.

"He was gone ten years except for the couple of times he came to New York when he was in school. When he came back after ten years, he had Ilse and the twins," Cartagena said as his cousin stopped in front of Cartagena's Riverside Drive building. "Thanks for listening, Pete," he said, patting Peter's knee. As he got out of the car he thought of telling Peter to give him a call sometime but knew it would be awkward when they met again. Peter was like all the Cartagena men, private and enigmatic. Cartagena didn't want to bury any more of them.

The rain had slackened but still fell in its originally hazy drizzle. The street lights in the park had come on. Feeling suddenly old, Cartagena went into the building, into the elevator and up to his apartment. Tired, he turned on the lights in the living room, went to the kitchen, pulled out a tray of ice from the refrigerator and headed for the bottle of scotch. Drink in hand, he sat in his soft reclining chair and stared at Raymond's painting.

After the third drink he decided he hated the painting and had only displayed it these many years as a matter of loyalty. He had never understood why his brother had wanted him to have it and why he derived so much enjoyment whenever he'd seen it on his visits to New York. Cartagena poured himself another drink and tried to fathom what was troubling him. An immense sorrow now enveloped him and his mourning felt much too personal.

He recalled hearing Raymond, late that last night, moving his suitcases down the stairs while his father started up the car to drive him to the airport. He had wanted it to be a dream but when he got up the next morning Raymond was gone. Feigning illness, he had refused to go to school and towards late afternoon left the house and walked alone on the beach. The sky had turned dark and the sea angry, the waves racing up on the shore to punish the pilings of the old pier. A few seagulls floated in the wind offshore but slowly drifted inland to seek refuge. Cartagena had sat down in the sand, feeling the storm coming as the air grew thicker and the colors changed, the sand itself becoming gray and the water lead-colored and knew only now that it had been his last day as a child.

REVENGE AND PRELUDE
TO A WELL-DESERVED SUICIDE

Riding out of the Port Authority Terminal on a Greyhound, George Cordero, wedded to America forever and betrayed by life once too many times, wrote in his journal:

> Nothing important to report. Still potted from magical Chiba-Chiba. Extreme paranoia. Next stop Philly. Mixed feelings about following her to coast after she took Bobby. Sense of foreboding. Will try to sleep. Mex on bus wants to get jug for trip. Going to Tulsa to see his mother. Looks more Spanish than Indian. Feeling of brotherhood. Must explore why. Seems honest while the other was shifty. Probable cause of suspicion: Nancy's secrecy about him. Still hurt by betrayal and lies about her involvement.

He was a fool and the world, overstocked with fools far too long, reminded him with every turn. And turns he made. He was like a child recently moved into a new neighborhood, wanting to fit in but not knowing how, waiting patiently at times, desperately at others for the initiation rites to be over. Such would never be the case for him. He would never belong. It was all too complicated. Some nights he remained awake attempting to decipher the source of his troubles, cursing himself and everyone about him, including his own son.

*   *   *

He had come close that summer. In the end, the secretary bird eluded him. She drowned him in a flood of tears down by the swimming pool, that place being his own kingdom, since it was he who each day primed the pump that carried water from the swampy stream into the swimming pool which he then treated with chlorine. It was a morning long process and the fat swamp frogs paid the price for his boredom. He noted then, in his already troubled mind, that the life expectancy of a bullfrog dropped into a gallon jar containing roughly one ounce

99

of powdered chlorine and four ounces of water was about forty-five seconds; he further noted that it took at least fifteen minutes to render that very same bullfrog to a pile of bleached white bones. Such had always been the hatred of himself and that ugliness which only he perceived.

But Alice Thompson could have changed all that. Sweet Alice Thompson with her curly blonde hair and flat chest, her lips constantly pursed as if she were playing the flute, which she loved doing while sitting alone in the tall grass beyond the ball field, the music drifting seemingly from the cool grass itself. God help her, he often thought now, if she ever found the other things she could do with her lovely red lips. She was a strange one. Arty he would christen her in later years when the word crept into his vocabulary. Breezy. There one minute and gone the next, exhaled like breath after a minor exertion, sighing like some chaste, prissy, nineteenth century schoolgirl, which she must have thought she was, bless her white puritan buttocks.

*   *   *

He was a mess. All the dreams were now gone, shattered against some invisible wall, destroyed. The only proof of his existence were the stains on his bed sheets where he masturbated nightly until sleep came. Out of habit, like a drunk who downs liquor mechanically, he grabbed his limp member and forcing it to perform, hating it like one hates a child, with tenderness, because the knowledge is there that children shouldn't be hated. But he forgot more often than not and stroked the flesh violently, autistically, needing to empty himself of desire. He was no longer able to conjure up a pretty face or a well-filled breast or even that magic triangle of pubic fleece which he detested even in pictures. He forced himself to drive out his devils by stroking vilely and at times allowing a forbidden thought to enter his mind, so that he saw either his body defiled by his wife's lover or imagined seeing the lover on top of her, and he entering that imaginary bedroom, gun in hand and forcing the lover to submit while on top of her. He would watch the horrified hag's face distorted by the pleasure of fear and the two heads, one reflecting satisfaction and the other pain.

He wanted the courage to destroy himself and pass into eternity defiantly, leaving his son to wonder about the mode of madness his father had chosen and at least making some impact in his life. To prolong his existence seemed a cruel joke. He was no better than his wife's father, his brain dissolved by alcohol, still reading college algebra texts as if the subject were the supreme mystery.

Part of the way to his destination, as he passed through the monotonous sameness that is America beyond its cities, George Cordero, new pilgrim thrown upon the shores of the promised land via a Pan Am flight from an island of coconuts and chirping tree frogs, wrote the introductory paragraph of a suicide letter to his son:

Dear Bobby,

I was a boy once. I was really. I was not a very happy boy. Not stupid either but not very smart. And I'm going to die. I don't know how soon but at some point I will stop living and things will go on being the same as they have always been. Yet I don't like it, just like I didn't like not understanding things when I was a boy. Things haven't changed that much since then. I don't know what dying is all about, but I'm going to find out soon.

He stopped writing as he drank coffee in Chicago. It was his fourteenth cup of coffee since leaving New York City. Through his sleepless haze, Cordero listened to the elevator English of his traveling companion, one Alejandro Jaramillo from Tulsa, Oklahoma, who urged him to at least have some apple pie, of all things. He shook his head slowly and refused, being careful to avoid moving too suddenly, lest his thoughts fall out and this fellow macho see his shame. Yet wanting desperately to divest himself of the burden and tell it all, confess his wife's escapade with the young superstud Chicano with whom they had double-dated. The stud had mocked his life with contrived friendship while he waited for Cordero to leave so he could resume Nancy's education of sexuality in the 70's. But Cordero had never been brave and instead of confiding in a stranger and letting his shame ebb away into the unimportance of table talk, his brain went on producing murderous schemes against his wife, so that whenever his mind's circuits overloaded with anger, his thoughts returned to his summer of thwarted desires.

*　　*　　*

Cordero hadn't understood Frank Medina's remorse when he confessed to the entire dormitory how and when he had relieved Helen, the Ukrainian Baptist, of her not so precious virginity. Frank had been contrite, had even cried over his deed and with a sincerity which left Cordero lacking, knelt on the floor to pray for deliverance from eternal damnation. While other young boys and girls at the Christian camp were groping left and right with fingers and tongues, he, like a monk, was tortured by guilt. Even his own sister, years later, confessed how wet she had been while necking with his friend, Paul Barton, who had gone on to become a Wall Street broker and no longer answered his phone calls.

Years later he had run into Frank peddling Mutual of Omaha. Frank had then bragged about his conquests that summer, including the elusive secretary bird, Sweet Alice Thompson. Only then did he understand what Frank's pious and teary confession had been about.

Cordero was a fool and the world was certainly overstocked and filled to the brim with fools. So it no longer mattered that he had touched Alice's private person, that he had felt the pink flesh parting under his probing finger, the triangle of blonde cocker spaniel fur grasping his finger like a Chinese finger puzzle.

*　　*　　*

Traveling through the night at 80 miles an hour in Plains country was like thrusting into space at rocket-ship speed. He counted the sleepless hours and they now amounted to 92. In this condition, his mind beginning to break up into weightless debris, Cordero, for the first time in his life, attempted the panacea of the insane.

He wrote a poem:

DEATH

A Vietnamese orphanage bombed.
I can't hear the screaming nor smell
the burning flesh.
An alcoholic cop is strangled,
chopped into seven pieces and stuffed
into a plastic bag.
Through the magic of television
6,000,000 Jews still die at Hitler's
hands each year.
Two tribes in Africa wipe each other out.
Bangladesh.
Biafra.
Lebanon.
Droughts and Plagues.
I feel no pain.
Death happens to everyone.

                                    *   *   *

At the campfire the flames ripped at the night and everyone sang: I'll sing you one-ho green grow the rushes ho. The air was cold on his face and he watched the others wrapped in twos under blankets. He roasted marshmallows on the burning logs and passed them on long sticks to the lovers. On the other side of the fire Alice Thompson looked like an apparition, her face aflame, her eyes far away, set apart from the others. Camp secretary. Separate room in the administration building, place at the camp director's table, same age as the rest of the counselors, caretakers and kitchen help, but set apart by her duties and her demeanor. She never danced the slow grinding music with the rest, never let the music and the dark starry nights affect her. He was drawn to Alice Thompson's aloofness, her seriousness, and wanted to find himself alone with her. He sensed she felt the same way, but would not advance, since it hadn't gone well with Juliet Dubzinski in the darkened recreation hall during the storm at the beginning of summer.

They had been dancing close, hardly moving, listening to the music and beyond it, the rain. The lights had gone out and the music stopped and they remained together, Juliet's body pressed against him, so that the hardness forced itself against her, his desire growing as they moved until the fluid rushed painfully from him, making him feel weak and helpless and turning his face hot with shame. He ran like he always would, ran from the pleasure and cursed Juliet for the whore she obviously was. For weeks he hated the slow music and, in reaction to that which had robbed him of his dignity, he played "Little Brown Jug" nineteen times in a row on the camp's victrola, driving everyone crazy except Kyle Engle, the camp bully, who joined him in the torture of withdrawal from "Blue Velvet," "Eddie, My Love," and "Earth Angel." Kyle, like Frank and Paul, was not a fool, but a slick, Four-F kind of a guy, Christian and everything, but he could drive-a-girl-bananas, the son of a bitch.

But not with Alice Thompson, even though the two of them were cut from the same mold. Wasps, they were now called at that time, but then they were just Americans, living in places like Scarsdale and Rye and Manhassett, names that clashed violently with their world of Simpson and Kelly Streets, Lexington Avenue, junkies, gangs, and the garbage and smells of the city. Not with Alice Thompson, he thought, because she was apart and unreachable. Like him, she was arrested in her social development, an atavism of morality, so that she became a joke. They called her the secretary bird, she was so spindly and flat-chested, with a face that was sorrow in its purest form. She was pretty, really, but sad, her eyes veiled by some unexplainable pain.

That night at the campfire they had all laughed and called her the name. She cried and he laughed at the joke, not sure why he was laughing.

*   *   *

When Alejandro Jaramillo said goodbye in Tulsa, it was the second day of George Cordero's space travel. He watched the flat land and the sun burning everything it touched, feeling as if he were standing still and the landscape were rolling by on a fast moving screen. Sleep began to intrude, but he fought it and resumed writing to his son.

> Mr. Drucker down the hall died the other day. He was a fine man, a fine Yiddish writer who survived a place called the Warsaw ghetto and wrote about it. He died and they took his body to Israel. His daughter said it was better that way because it stopped his suffering. He was a tough man, Mr. Drucker. God bless him. On the elevator he often told me how screwed up America was and how much people were being damaged by power and selfishness. He knew about such things and now he's dead. And my father, your grandfather's dead. Twelve years now. You were only five months in your mother when he died. He left and four months later you showed up. I kept thinking it was like turning in an old car for a new one. You remind me of him with your carvings and madness,

but I don't like to talk about him, so I won't. I wish the two of you
had met and talked to kind of pass things on, because I'm not too
good at that type of thing. I don't know what this world is about.
Please forgive me, but I really don't. I keep trying to figure it out,
but I think I'm one of those people who will never understand life.

I don't want you to be afraid when you read this. Death happens
to everyone. It doesn't matter how it comes. I don't want to give
up, but I can't figure out if going on is important enough. I've been
told I'm a good teacher, but it isn't a good enough reason. I don't
know how to teach people to save themselves from themselves and
that's what they want to learn.

George Cordero stopped writing and made a new determination to stay awake
and not miss seeing Texas. In Amarillo he remained on the bus. On the edge
of sleep he dreamed-thought that he had made up with his wife, waited until one
day when the surf was up, and took her to Venice Beach. As they played in the
water, he'd drag her down and try to drown her. He'd hold his foot on her chest
and call for help, but it would be too late by the time anyone heard him above the
roaring waves. He discarded the idea, knowing there would be questions about
the scratches on his legs and the traces of his flesh under her fingernails. A rush
of intense hatred momentarily blinded him and he closed his eyes. The bus was
moving again and he felt sleep invade his body, but he stiffened against it and
was once again awake, staring at the dry, desolate rangeland. He still loved his
wife and the knowledge hurt more than any of her betrayals. Why had he always
picked women who couldn't give themselves to him?

*   *   *

When the laughter died down they began singing, in the cool starry night,
"John Jacob Hinklehammersmith, his name was my name too," the voices fading
with each stanza, only to rise in tumult like the flames of the campfire suddenly
fanned by a gust of wind: "DA-DA-DA-DA-DA-DA-DA-DAH ... "

To this day he still did not know where the courage had come from but he
remembered that he felt sorry for Alice Thompson. He stood up and crossed
over to the other side of the campfire and, wrapped in his own blanket, he sat
next to her and asked her what was the matter, to which she replied that it was
nothing. He pressed her but she shook her head and got up. With her blanket
wrapped around her like an old Indian, so that the sight created further comedy,
she began climbing the hill to the road.

"Where are you going?" he shouted.

"To bed," she said.

"Wait for me," he called, unconsciously, not recognizing why the others were
suddenly shouting and whistling, the girls giggling. "Wait up," he said as he ran
up after her, the applause and cheers lapping at his ears, making them hot. He

was now the hunter of the elusive secretary bird. Walking down the hill in the crisp air of that late summer evening with the moon just beginning to rise, he felt deliciously vicious. Like a junior vampire, he thought. Frank Medina used to imitate Bela Lugosi: "Don't be frightened, darlink. All I vant to do is trink your blood. Pull down your panties." He put his arm around her shoulder and, wrapped in their blankets, they bounced down the hill. Two old Indians going directly to Hell. Do not pass Gomorrah and pray to the Almighty that He doesn't catch you cunnilingus flagrante, which years later he had given the bitch, Nancy Covington, his brazen, witch-of-a-bitch-of-a-wasp wife to her heart's content, as the price she exacted for allowing him within.

"Hey, I'm sorry about laughing back there," he said.

"It's okay, I'm just edgy," she answered nervously.

"Why?"

"No reason. Listen, you should go back up."

"It's all right. I don't belong up there either."

"Suit yourself."

Going past the pagoda, he took her hand. She didn't resist.

"Alice?" he said, his voice nearly inaudible as he spoke her name. "Let's go to the pool."

"What for?"

"I have to check the pump," he lied.

"I'll wait for you."

"It won't take long."

She allowed herself to be led through the tall grass and raspberry bushes and waited by the pines at the edge of the pool. When he returned from the pump shack and his lie, which consisted of banging a wrench against a pipe a couple of times, he put his arms around her from behind and nuzzled her hair as he'd seen in a movie.

"Let's not go back yet," he said.

"I should."

"We'll just sit and talk, please."

He opened his blanket and spread it on the grass and they sat. The excitement, not the cold, made him shiver. She opened her blanket, let him in and, closed-lipped, they kissed twice. The third time his tongue slipped out, first across her lips and then to her beautiful teeth, so that he felt as if he were licking a dish. She tore violently away from him, lowered her head and began to cry.

"I'm sorry," he said.

"It's my fault," she said, drying her eyes.

She touched his face and awkwardly he lay her down, his hands going immediately to her chest to find only disappointment. Expecting softness, he instead confronted buttons and undergarments. She began crying again, her shoulders heaving and her voice so hurt and full of embarrassment that he wanted to run away. It was as if he had committed a greater sin than he had with Juliet, which in fact he had, being he was a fool.

"We can go steady," he almost shouted, his voice seemingly echoing in the darkness, ebbing away, so that it clashed with the singing voices drifting down from the campfire. 'A hundred bottles of beer on the wall, a hundred bottles of beer . . . ' "Really, we can," he added more softly as if to appease her, bribe her for his transgression.

"Please don't say that unless you mean it," she said.

"I mean it, Alice, please."

"Don't."

"I've always wanted to go steady with you."

"I can't."

"Is it because I'm Spanish?" he said.

"No, that doesn't matter," she said, dolefully.

"Why, then?"

"I'm no good," she whimpered. "If you really knew about me, you wouldn't even talk to me."

"Tell me."

"I can't."

And then he tried kissing her again and she almost gave in to that Gallic mystery which for the past three years had been his obsession; she had almost opened her teeth, which were clamped shut. Instead, she drew back and shook her head violently like a flea-bitten dog, her blonde hair flying in his face. She stood up and gathered up her blanket, and shot off through the grass with him following. He caught her at the bridge, which ran over the small stream, where one subsequent summer morning when everyone in the camp had gone to the quadrangle to get ready for lunch and he had just finished adding the day's portion of chlorine to the pool, he happened on five snakes sunning themselves on the flat rocks in the middle of the stream. With ancestral fear and disgust running in his veins, he methodically dropped a large rock into their midst, causing writhing and bloodshed among his primeval enemies. He was convinced that the defenseless snakes had emitted tiny sounds of pain. He laughed nervously at his mind's joke: Me Adam you Snake.

He grabbed Alice Thompson forcefully and pushed her body against the lead pipes of the bridge; kissed her again until she yielded to him, her open mouth nearly liquid, so that he felt as if he were drinking a long sought after elixir. She seemed like a hungry child then and tasted sweet and as if she had been chewing on fresh morning grass. His head light and his mind spinning from the sensation, he led her away from the bridge to the underbrush beneath the row of pines and there, very slowly, as in a dream, he explored her thighs and belly, working his hands up and down until he was there, finding the tiny orifice. For years his only memory of a woman was that night; he wanted somehow to relive the sensation even after he had gorged himself on the flesh of five-dollars-a-shot Portuguese whores.

He could've gone further with Alice that night, but Frank never told him until years later when he tried to sell him a policy. When his desperate and awkward gropings and her equally desperate attempts at chastity were over and he was aching from the struggle, they walked back to the quadrangle, their arms around each other, wrapped in the two blankets like some monster hulk bumping along in the night. When they came to the edge of the dormitory, area she said goodnight and ran off. He remained sitting on the steps of the recreation hall, watching the stars, mesmerized by the dark vastness and more than ever convinced that he had been created to suffer.

*   *   *

Traveling through the heart of Texas, the rangeland spreading to the horizon, here and there dotted by clumps of brush and a scattered gathering of skeletal longhorns, George Cordero, betrayed associate professor of psychology, continued writing to his already crazed son, who at the age of twelve did not yet read well enough to withstand school and spent hours on end carving oddly shaped figures from scraps of wood. Like himself, his son was intractably committed to the notion that the entire universe had been created solely to deprive him of pleasure.

He wrote:

> I have no country, no clear identity. I've tried to identify with humanity, but it doesn't work. We're some strange phenomenon too difficult to comprehend. We make progress as a species, but with each step we grow crazier. Each refinement produces greater arrogance in the face of catastrophe. Now we have decided to invade the stars. I can't imagine you going off to live in the stars, but I suppose it will happen. If not you, then your son. Stars at night are so beautiful, especially in the mountains of the island where as a child I grew up dumbfounded by its beauty. There, in Cacimar, there is no time. Life goes on pounding out the same rhythm each day. I wish I could have taken you up there just once. You and I could've been boys together.

After everyone returned from the campfire, he stood around as couples kissed goodnight and he knew nothing would come of his time grappling with Alice Thompson. That had been it. The next morning it was as if nothing had happened between them. Alice went on performing her duties and he went on performing his. As if the entire adult and teenage population of the camp had known of his failure and were too embarrassed for him, no one commented on their exit from the campfire. No one kidded him about his hunting of the elusive secretary bird. Frank and Paul acted as if the previous night had been skipped. The joke had run its course. When the summer ended they dispersed to different parts of the state and he returned to the city and its squalor. There, he put the two months at Oaks and Pines Christian Camp in the pain storage of his mind. But in the middle of September he received a letter from Alice. Curleycued and fragrant, the lilac stationery spoke rhapsodically about their evening, causing him to hear musical sounds rising from the paper and forcing him to see her injured, sorrowed face. He wrote back and told her that he was going into the Air Force in December and would she continue writing to him. He signed the letter love, as she had. He hoped she would cry. The following week there was a letter from the other girl, Juliet Dubzinski. The writing, the script as well as the thoughts, were totally uncomplicated. She talked about their friendship and how sad and wasteful it was, because by all rights they should've fallen in love, and how badly she'd wanted to be his girl. The letter forced him to recall the night of his accident, remembering that even after he'd run off and left her puzzled by his actions, she still sought him out and invited him to the movies and on a hayride and walks down by the lake. He'd made excuses to Juliet because Tommy Morales had staked a claim on her and it was against the code to tamper with a friend's girl, although there were exceptions, but he had yet to figure out how to go about it; recalling that he'd wanted her more than anything in his life, and when he thought about her he didn't think of murdering frogs or snakes or hatred of the unknown because she was beautiful and alive, full breasted and friendly, unafraid of boys and their brashness and peculiarities. His mind drifted back to the beginning of summer when they had met on the train on the way to camp and had liked each other immediately and laughed all the way to the camp. Later that very same night, they talked and for two weeks each time they saw each other they couldn't keep from laughing. At night, on the porch of the recreation hall, she sat on his lap like a big doll so that he could feel her pubic bone against his thigh, the two bones shifting against him when she straddled his leg and cuddled her breast against his face. The bone was actually the pubic symphisis, as he learned to call the two bones after a year of anatomy courses, which separated to allow a newborn his first sensation of otherness, of fear, and the future. She called him her big brother, her sweet breath coming and going, talking softly about dreams and wishes; they were silly words emitted more from her brilliant, nighttime cat eyes than from her lips.

He was torn by his two loves then, not choosing one over the other, but riding them out in nights of torture and regret until at the end of November, Juliet wrote. No longer employing the upside down stamp, and signing herself his friend, she informed him that she had become engaged to a sailor and that was the end of that. Alice continued writing, long descriptive passages of autumn and her emotions, everything thoughtfully constructed and through it, the sadness adding depth and shadow to her words.

Even after he was in the Air Force she continued writing two letters each week for two years. He wrote back, emulating her style, the subdued tones, the landscape and weather, his emotions mirroring her own. At times he felt as if he were reading one of her letters rather than writing to her. And all the while he vented his anger sexually on the diminutive whores of Terceira Island of the Azores group in the Atlantic, where he was stationed; at times play-acting as in masturbation, imagining that he was making love to Juliet Dubzinski, never Alice Thompson, and under his breath calling out her name. Eventually, he grew tired of Alice Thompson's musical letters and one day, in impotent, angry language, he cursed flutes and Oberlin College, where she'd gone, and that ended that relationship forever.

* * *

On the Texas-New Mexico border, in a Mexican restaurant, George Cordero, stubble-faced, gaunt, nearly hallucinating from lack of sleep, drank coffee once more and spoke to a leathery, reptilian-looking cowboy about rope tricks and knots. He got back on the bus and finished writing his goodbye letter to his son. He wrote:

> I don't like Americans, Bobby. I don't mean I dislike every American, but that I don't like what happens to people in this country. I don't like it at all, but I can't do anything about it. I'll be going soon. Take care of yourself and always remember that I tried to love you and your mother, but didn't know how.
>
> > Your father,
> > George

On the third night of his voyage into space, George Cordero arrived at space station 87 outside of Gallup, New Mexico, his mind a shower of meteors hurtling through time. He bought a stamp from a silver and bluestone Indian salesgirl and mailed his letter. He guessed it would arrive the day after he did. By that time it would be all over. He got back on the bus and slept through Arizona and a good part of California, waking up only when the rhythm of the bus shifted from the open highway to the Los Angeles freeway traffic.

When he arrived in Santa Monica, he dragged himself from the bus, took a cab and arrived at the house which his wife had rented in Venice. She and his son were eating supper when he arrived. Her face went pale beneath the tanned skin of her California front and she rushed to him crying that she was sorry. The boy went on eating as if his four month absence had been a trip to the corner to purchase cigarettes.

That night when he and his wife were alone, he raped her brutally. She cried and then he questioned her about the lover, each detail adding to his madness until he could no longer contain himself and he made her cut her long blonde hair and pull out every piece of clothing she had ever worn when she was with her lover. With the pile of clothes and her hair, he marched her to the backyard and made her burn everything in an oil drum, convinced that he was no longer insane, but was in touch with some ancient rite of purification. He raped her again and then slept until late in the day. When he woke up, he checked the mailbox and found the letter he'd written to his son on the trip and a note from his wife saying that she and the boy had gone to the beach and would return around four. He ripped up the letter to his son and placed it in the garbage, covering it up with discarded wrappers and cans. It would serve no purpose to injure him. His battle was with her and once again the anger flowed in his system. He wanted to crush something, to obliterate it so thoroughly that no traces were left. Deep within him a voice cried out for reason, for restraint. But it was a faint voice, weak and without conviction, devoid of power. What had she said last night? We can try again. Maybe a child, another child. That was it. She'd become pregnant and wanted to protect herself. And again the voice, weakly, told him that the fight was over, that her contriteness was real this time, that more than ever they were wedded forever, bonded through touch and smell, and she would never again leave him. The constancy which he'd wished for had finally come and his madness and brutality had been of little consequence in her choice, because finally she'd seen the extent of his pain. But it wasn't enough.

Slowly, his mind screening out all emotion, listening neither to the superficial madness nor to the thread of reason which still remained, George Cordero went to his son's room and searched until he found one of the knives. He tested the fine razor-like edge, a thin line of steel so delicate that it appeared fragile, sharper, however, than the scalpels he'd used in dissections so many years ago. He knew there would be pain, but he could bear it. He's seen it done many times as a boy, on pigs and bulls, the men's motion swift and effortless. For a moment he wondered about the bleeding. Would he be able to stop it in time?

His mind visualized the act, sorting out the anatomy until he was certain where he'd have to cut, the impetus of his decision separating fear from will.

In the bathroom, he locked the door and removed his clothes. He mustn't panic now, otherwise he'd botch it up and butcher himself. It would be all right afterwards. They'd make up and then for years when they made love she'd feel the absence. Because eventually they'd make love again somehow. After he cleansed himself they'd make love. The thought aroused him and he again blanked his mind and sat on the open toilet seat, waiting until the desire subsided.

Orchids, he thought. From the Greek. Pertaining to the testicles. What was the operation called? Dr. Friedlander had told him about the study on the Rhesus monkeys on Cayo Santiago, off the beach at Humacao, in Puerto Rico. He said Maxwell was working on the project. If Cordero happened to go down there he ought to look Maxwell up, since they had been classmates in graduate school. Cayo Santiago was a small island with nothing but the Rhesus monkeys on it. Its sole purpose was to breed Rhesus for experiments all over the United States.

The people in the project had performed the operation on a couple of dozen monkeys, both males and females. He remembered now. In females it was an ovariectomy and in males an orchiectomy. After the operations the animals were sterile but went on feeling desire. He had gone with Maxwell to Cayo Santiago. Tony Maxwell was from Wyoming and couldn't stop raving about the incredible colors of the water, the beauty of Puerto Rico. Why would anyone want to leave such a paradise, Maxwell had asked, shaking his head.

Cordero had been fascinated by the insane behavior of the monkeys. Their scientific name was Macaca Mulatta. The screeching and aimless running around after one another unnerved him. Their hysteria made him feel as if he were back in high school and could do nothing about the bullies who tormented him. The sound of the name made him laugh. He thought he knew a song about a mulatta named Catalina, but that had been long ago, and heard himself chuckle from far away. Cayo Santiago was like a miniature of the big island, the monkeys sharing only three concerns: eating, screwing and fighting to establish a hierarchy of authority.

Some years later there was wide-spread sterilization of women in Puerto Rico. As many as 250,000 women, if not more, were sterilized as they had done with the female monkeys. The operation, however, was not performed on any men. Cordero had heard that the in joke among the Americans on that project was that it wasn't necessary, since the men had already given up their balls to the U.S. All of that was politics and had nothing to do with him. What he was about to do was different, he reassured himself. She, the bitch, Nancy, wanted to trap him to cover up for having someone else's child. He'd show her.

The first cut was tentative, awkward, the thin blade burning the skin and his hands coming away stained. His mind traveled back through the maze of knowledge: Physiology, Anatomy, Biology until he saw the diagram he was looking for. He saw it clearly, outlined in reds and blues: Vas deferens, Epididymis, Seminiferous tubules. The cut had to be clean, final. How had they done it? The men in his childhood who laughed at the pigs' squealings. They pulled first, pulled down on the scrotum. He pulled until he felt the pain deep inside of him and then ran his son's carving knife forcefully in one motion across the taut skin which she had at one time so tenderly caressed. So violent had been the action that he cut himself on the opposite thigh. He held the warm, raw egg mass in his hand for a moment without looking at it and then let it slither into the toilet bowl, his mind screaming with the agony. His eyes closed, he flushed the toilet, the rush of water invading his mind like a thunderous cascade.

He now held a towel to the wound and waited, frightened for the first time that he'd bleed to death. Pressure, that was the important thing. There was a moment when he thought he would pass out from the pain, but after a few moments it subsided. He removed the towel and felt the folds of skin, tingling now to his touch. The bleeding had stopped, but the pain was now becoming greater. It traveled upward, making his head heavy, his face hot, the cold sweat pouring out of his skin. Suddenly, he recalled there was one artery that was connected directly to the aorta. He couldn't recall its name. If he'd severed the artery, it had now snapped back into the abdominal cavity and he was bleeding internally. The nausea fought its way up and he leaned over the bowl and vomited. The two oblong masses had returned and were staring back at him like the blinded eyes of some monster creature which threatened to rise up out of the scarlet water to devour him. They made him feel like a young child. He flushed the toilet once more, mopped the floor with the towel, rinsed it, wrung it out, washed the sink and raced to put on his clothes. The room was spinning violently now and the blackness came twice before he managed to unlock the bathroom door and stagger to the phone. Through the haze which was now invading his mind he gave the operator the address to the house and waited for the ambulance to arrive.

He blacked out for a moment. When he came to he could hear the ambulance arrive and the door open. Through the gauze-like reality that reminded him of the mosquito nets on the island, he perceived the attendants examining him. Behind them, as he lay on the floor, he saw a woman and a boy, but could not recognize them. She reminded him of his wife. The boy looked remarkably like himself when he was growing up, but that was impossible. He was a grown man, a psychologist, a professor, a PhD with many articles on the effects of tropical foods on the human brain. She appeared to be friendly and listened attentively while he told her that he would be okay, that he was just passing through. She seemed frightened but he couldn't figure out why. There was a faint perception that he'd seen her somewhere before, long ago, but he couldn't recall where. As the darkness began enveloping George Cordero for the last time, he thought that perhaps she might be a doctor or perhaps she played the flute, but he wasn't quite sure.

THE KITE

As if his office were a giant magnet which attracted neighborhood hysteria, his day invariably began with a frantic call from one of his clients. There was no translator at the Welfare Department; the nurse at the Public Health Clinic had made them return home for their clinic card even though she knew them by name; and crime of crimes, the building inspector had arrived too early, and naturally, he didn't expect to get in, with the apartment still in that condition. It never stopped. Like waves upon a shore, they buffeted his conscience with their helpless demands. Their voices heavy, they clung desperately to him.

This time the phone call was not from a client but from his own mother, concerned again about his father's health. "It's his heart, Ricky," she said, tremulously, adding that his father had complained of chest pains the previous week, and she'd made him go to Kings County Hospital for a checkup. She paused and, holding back her tears, told him the doctors had suggested he take it easy for a few months. "He can't go lifting heavy things in the job," she said. "They laid him off yesterday, Ricky. *Le dieron leiof.*" His mother pronounced the word *issy*, and compulsively he corrected her. "Easy, Ma," he said. "And on the job. Not in the job."

"*Sí, m'ijito,*" she replied, becoming self-conscious and lapsing totally into Spanish.

"Did you tell Becky?" he asked.

"*No, todavía no.*"

"Why not, Ma?"

"*No quiero que tenga problemas con la criatura,*" she explained she hoped Becky would not have problems with the baby. He said he understood but silently wished she hadn't reminded him of his clients. The following day Mrs. Ramos and her daughter, Amy, were due in his office to plan a strategy for letting Mr. Ramos know that his daughter, at age fifteen, was pregnant and had no way of determining who had "given her the baby." That's what Amy had said, as if babies were acquired in much the same manner as the common cold. From the sublime to the ridiculous with something lost in translation.

113

His sister Rebecca was due to have her second child and his mother didn't want her to have problems with the creature. He wanted to be sympathetic but felt only annoyance and consequently guilt. As he listened to his mother, his temples began throbbing, a sure sign of an upcoming tension headache. In a nightmarish fantasy which he recognized as a Kafkaesque indulgence on his part, it seemed as if the green-gray institutional walls of his small office, decorated with posters in English and Spanish, warning and exhorting on the perils of venereal disease, unwanted pregnancy, tooth decay, drugs, and a poor diet, were closing in on him, rendering him a felon condemned to spend the rest of his life doling out advice on how people could work themselves up from the morass of their lives. He didn't want to think about it. His mother was going on about the difficulty of his sister's last pregnancy.

"That's okay, Ma," he said, a bit shrilly. "I'll call Becky if you want."

"No, no," she answered. "Don't worry. It's all right. Just come tonight, Ricky. Come and visit. Sit down and have supper with your father. I'll make *chuletas* and *tostones* the way you both like them."

"Okay, Ma. I'll be there after work," he said, and held back from saying that the fried food was killing his father.

"What time?" she said.

"About seven, Ma."

"No school tonight?"

"No, no school, Ma," he said. "*Bendición.*"

"*Qué Dios te bendiga, m'ijito,*" she said, blessing him. Rick Sánchez hung up the phone and for the rest of the day, as he attempted to bring some order to other people's lives, at times vacillating between despair and anger, he thought about his father: busting himself up year after year, handling heavy scrap metal in winter and summer so that his hands were cracked, the fingers twisted, the fingernails crushed and grown over. And when he picked up his guitar to play his *décimas*, he looked like a trained brown bear, except that his face took on a look of such kindness that Rick felt like he was ten again, walking hand in hand with him on the boardwalk in Coney Island, never afraid because his Papi was there with his big muscles, holding him tight on the roller coaster rising and falling so that the ocean looked tilted and the sky so close he could almost touch it. Papi, make a muscle. Show Juanny and Pito. Show 'em, Papi. Busting himself up inside all those years so his kids could go to college, foregoing that psychically ubiquitous dream house on the island to pay for books and clothes and later a few bucks for him, his only son, *sangre de mi sangre y alma de mi alma*, bloodofmyblood and soulofmysoul. Extra *cocos* for him to entertain the ladies, like he said, winking knowingly, or seemingly so, as he put on his air of macho around town, but not fooling anyone, because there had never been another woman since he'd met Rick's mother in Cacimar, up there in the mountains, and had serenaded her until, hat in hand, twisting and sweating, he had asked for her hand in marriage and then had promised to love her and keep her in sickness and in health and all the other hallowed garbage, Rick thought.

Thinking and wishing, as he traveled the maze of other people's pain, that his father could finally understand that they were not the same men and that too much had happened in the passage from one culture into the other. He wanted desperately to convey his respect but the words always came out short and angry, so full of the New York wise guy that even after Psychology and Sociology, and Freud and Jung, and Sartre and Camus, and the rest of the booknames, the distance was still there between them. And now his father was ready to check out forever without a resolution to their differences.

Numbed by the knowledge that he might soon be faced with the paradox of freedom brought on by grief, Rick Sánchez, as if in sleep, listened mechanically to the faceless voices and called, and referred, and counseled until he finished his daily penance. He left work aching. Not only his head, but his entire body felt as if it had absorbed each single pain brought to him. Out in the street he walked in a daze, the gray tenements echoing his own helpless cry for release from the daily agony of existing among tortured souls.

Once on the subway he tried amusing himself by wondering why "Only the Dead Know Brooklyn," a favorite short story by Thomas Wolfe. Deeper and deeper into Brooklyn and into himself he went, listening, watching, as he grew closer to home, the waters of the Atlantic, winter dark, the sky too gray to describe at day's end, identifying the responsibilities of impending death, categorizing major and minor anxieties, minimizing guilt while doors opened and closed and opened and the train click-clacked over the rails, click-clacking to keep the beat for swarms of pushing, squirming, dying people, until exhausted, more by not knowing what awaited him than from the hour-long ride, he bolted upright and rode the last few stops standing, anticipating the hatred he now felt towards the crass amusement park of his childhood, so desolate in winter, his memories like shadows thrown upon the wall of time.

He walked quickly down the stairs of the elevated train platform, despising the street, the shuttered game booths and smells of warmed-over quick food. The voices of his innocence were calling him, beckoning him to his childhood, lulling him so he felt as if he'd drown in anxiety before he arrived. He knew there was to be no respite once he reached his father's home and yet he felt not as harried and therefore more conscious that he was trapped and was being asked to return to a kind of amusement park called Spicland, where one took rides and played games of chance in Spanish.

In the elevator of the massive housing project, he thought about the Ramos' case, wondering if his father would've understood Rebecca becoming pregnant at fifteen. When he rang the doorbell his mother immediately opened the door. This confirmed his suspicion that she was watching the street and had timed his arrival. He asked her for her blessing, received it and kissed her dutifully. "Where's Pop?" he asked, expecting to be informed that he was in the bedroom, resting.

"He's in the kitchen peeling the *plátanos* for the *tostones*," his mother said, wiping her hands on her apron and closing the door. She was thin and small and finally, in the last year, she was beginning to look old, her dark skin a little wrinkled and her fine, Indian hair, once so black, beginning to gray. "You know how he is," she added in Spanish, excusing his presence in the kitchen. "He's got to be moving his hands all the time." Rick laughed self-consciously and let out a big breath. When he had taken off his overcoat and loosened his tie, he called out, "How you doing, Pop?" wanting his father's voice to reassure him before he saw the man and had to take in any change in him.

"I'm all right, Rick," his father answered. "C'mon in and have a beer."

Rick crossed the neat, linoleum-covered living room, the furniture like that inside a showcase: lamps, tables, shelves, figurines, plaster bullfighters and ballerinas on the walls, sofa and chairs, straight out of some unpublished Latin "House Beautiful" or "Better Homes and Fire Escapes" magazine; cheap, expensive-looking furniture which offered some semblance of unconscious upward mobility, a concept which his parents would never understand, just like they did not understand middle class or ethnic. New Yorkers were either Irish, Jewish, Italian, Chinese or Negro. The rest were Puerto Ricans, acknowledging other Latins as mere extensions, latecomers who spoke the language, albeit oddly, and therefore fell into that all encompassing category of *hispanos*. Kathy, the cornfed blonde VISTA volunteer from Iowa, whom he had brought to dinner to satisfy their curiosity and hers, had baffled his mother. When asked if Bauer were an Irish name, Kathy had responded that it was German. His mother had nodded politely but with undisguised incredulity—as if to point out that Kathy need not be ashamed of her background, at least not in her house—commented that it was funny but that Kathy looked Irish. In her scheme of things, blondes and redheads were Irish, brunettes Italians, and the ones who weren't black and obviously not Latin, were Jewish. So much for the melting pot theory, a concept which his mother had never encountered, but had nevertheless mastered.

"How you making out, Pop?" Rick said, as he took a seat at the other end of the table, opposite his father.

"You know. Working," his father said. Then he laughed, embarrassed by his choice of words. "Well, not right now. But I keep busy talking to your mother. She likes to hear me talk about the old country."

Having worked on the Brooklyn docks and for the last ten years with the metal company, his father used the phrase as if he were a European immigrant. And when he said "the old country," his eyes took on the same wistful look of the man who has admitted he has been seduced by America, not resenting his folly because life had been good in some respects, and this was all a man could ask for, but wishing once more for youth and therefore connecting the desire to the homeland. But he hadn't changed. There was not a trace of whatever the doctors had found. He looked strong as ever, the neck muscled and his dark eyes deep and narrow above his hawk nose. He was lighter than his mother but being out in the sun had burnished his skin to a permanent bronze.

"You know what I mean, Rick?"

"Yeah, I understand, Pop," Rick said, emptily. Wanting to change the conversation, he asked how his younger sister was doing in school.

"She's doing good, Ricky," his father said. Without turning away from the stove his mother said that Christina had gone downstairs to finish her homework with her friend Elizabeth.

"She coming up soon?" His mother stopped stirring the pot of beans, looked at the clock on the wall, nodded and resumed stirring. As if she were simply making small talk, she asked if Rick had ever met his sister's girlfriend. "They just moved into the building," she said. Ever on the alert, his father caught on immediately.

"For Chrisake, Margarita," he said. "Leave him alone. He's only twenty-six." Rick searched for sarcasm in his father's remark but found none. "Geez, I didn't have the guts to ask for your hand until I was a year older."

"She goes to Hunter College with Christina," his mother went on, paying no attention to his father's reproach of her matchmaking. "She wants to be a kindelgalden teacher."

"Ma, she's a baby," Rick protested. "What is she, nineteen? She's Chris' age, right?"

There had been no malice in the words but there was little doubt in Rick's mind that his father was enjoying his discomfort. He laughed and, pointing the long knife at him, told him to watch out. "It's a conspiracy," he said. "You don't know it but they get together late at night and decide who's going to get this guy or that one. You can't get away from them. You can go anywhere you want and think they ain't gonna find you, but they do. They're worse than the CIA. How do you think they got me? If it wasn't for the conspiracy I'd be a free man today."

His father had finished paring the thick skin off the plantains, sliced them diagonally and placed the slices into two bowls of salted water. The green ones went into one and the ripe into the other. With a deft motion of the knife he swept the plantains skins off the table and into a garbage bag and, standing up, asked Rick if he wanted a beer. Rick asked if he was going to have one.

"*¡Seguro que sí!*" he said. "This thing with the heart is nothing," he added, pounding his chest with the palm of his hand. "Your mother probably told you I was ready for the grave. Whatta they gonna do, open me up and gimme a new engine?"

Over his father's broad shoulders, Rick looked at his mother. Her eyes wore a pleading look and Rick knew she was repeating a silent prayer. Rick answered quickly that all she had said was that he needed rest.

"That was all, Pop."

"C'mon," his father said in Spanish, handing him a can of beer. "Let's go sit in the living room. If we stay here people are gonna start saying your mother's got me sitting on the trunk." He said all of it in Spanish, adopting the fraudulent, tough guy image, the reference to the trunk being the equivalent of the henpecked husband. Rick followed his father into the living room and sat down on the couch. His father took the big chair opposite him. For a while they said nothing. Rick could hear the frying in the kitchen, the smells wafting to him in waves of memories of cold winters, before they moved into the projects, when he would race home in the twilight of evening, zooming up the four flights of the tenement and sniffing always, like an animal, not consciously but instinctively, so that even were he blind he could've reached home on the aroma of his mother's cooking, on time each day, no matter what meat it was except on Thanksgiving, always with rice, white, red, mixed with beans or *gandules*, even black rice, black from the ink of the *calamares*, the canned squid, and beans in sauce, *salsa*, like the music now, thick and spicy, making you forget disappointments.

They sat in silence still, two strangers. Outside, darkness had taken over and way out on the channel a boat was making its way out to sea, the lights of its superstructure shimmering like tear drops over the dark water. A *marintaiga*, Rick thought. The "Marine Tiger" returning unhappy victims of an experiment back to their homeland. It was a make-believe ship which traveled in his consciousness bringing spics from the island to the city. He'd never seen the ship, had never met anyone who admitted having arrived on it; everyone always claimed entrance into the great land on Eastern or Pan Am; the ship thus passed from the reality of its dank, crowded quarters and rough seas, to the level of myth. And yet he recalled the word *marintaiga* being used in *bodegas*, in school, outside the church on Sundays, at parties, playgrounds, and in the halls of his adolescence when he was undecided about accepting the *yerba*, the sweet smelling smoke which seemed as much a part of their existence as the language he shared with the others. The word was applied to the ship primarily, but also to any newly arrived person whose English was inadequate or whose manner was backward. They were now called hicks. The *marintaiga* had vanished and in its place hicks now graced the landscape, their faces still sallow, their bodies still small and undernourished, the pencil-thin mustaches razor-sharp, the Yardley-slick, brilliantined haircuts singling them out as outcasts, their funny black and white shoes, the mud of that wretched island still encrusted on them, making them caricatures to be ridiculed. They bred each year and reproduced hip, sophisticated, English-speaking replicas of themselves, males and females, their eyes hungry and pleading.

His father finally broke the silence by asking about Kathy Bauer, how he was doing with her. He said he guessed she was all right, that he had stopped seeing her at the end of the summer and that she had gone home the previous month. His father seemed surprised and then the corners of his mouth turned down, his brows went up and he nodded, reflecting for a moment before he took another sip of beer.

"She was a little silly, wasn't she?" he said, smoothing his mustache with the back of his hand. "*Boba*, you know, Ricky. *Medio apendejá.*"

Rick laughed in earnest. For the time being the ice had been broken and things were forgiven between them. One thing about the old man, Rick thought, he had guts. "Yeah, Pop," he said, truly having no argument with his father's assessment of Kathy. "She was a little silly."

"I'm not kidding," his father said, confidentially, leaning forward in his seat. "I'm speaking to you man to man. You need a strong woman. You know, no crap. All business. The house and the kids." He sounded like one of his Italian buddies from the docks of South Brooklyn. "You wanna woman you can respect. Somebody you don't have to worry about watching where she goes and who she talks to. Me, I was lucky with your Ma."

"I understand, Pop," he said.

"I know you understand, Rick," his father replied, leaning back once more as if the effort had tired him. He reflected a moment, choosing his words. "I wasn't mad at you for living with the girl. Not even your mother was mad. We understand how things change and young people want freedom. In my day freedom was being able to pick your own clothes or the kind of trade you wanted to take up. Your mother and me may not have an education like you but we're not stupid people. It wasn't even that she was an American."

"I know, Pop."

"You believe me, right? I'm not prejudiced, you know that. You brought all your friends to the house. Negro, white, Jewish. I didn't care. People are people. Some are good and some are rotten. But silly women are nothing but trouble and in that the color doesn't matter."

"I guess I found out the hard way," Rick said, relenting, avoiding the argument.

"Sometimes that's the only way," his father said, nodding philosophically. "That's why I didn't say nothing to you. I wasn't happy about you and the girl but I wasn't mad at you. Why did she go home?"

"I don't know. I guess breaking up with me had something to do with it. I think the neighborhood finally got to her. She thought she was really going to solve the problems on her block. You know, the drugs and illegitimate kids and the rest of the crap. It was too much for her. Hell, it's too much for the people themselves, let alone some young kid who's been sheltered all her life and the only time she ever saw people who weren't white was in the movies."

"You miss her?"

"At first. You know, you get used to a woman."

"Yeah, I know." His father was agreeing but the subject was obviously causing him discomfort. The generalization included him and therefore his own relationship to Rick's mother. "She was a good looking girl, that was for sure," he said, perhaps regretting, or so Rick conjectured, that he had been the cause of the breakup between him and Kathy. He realized the speculation was made only to soothe himself and the impotent anger he had experienced when he didn't tell his father to tend to his own affairs.

He wasn't able to explore the feeling, for at that moment the door of the apartment swung open and Christina came in, trailed by another girl. His sister was a young replica of their mother: small, thin, pretty in a kind of acceptable way, attractive to males but not threatening to women. In contrast to the almost bland nature of their mother, however, Christina was full of their father's brash enthusiasm. Her eyes opened and she let out a squeal of delight upon seeing Rick. Before he had a chance to greet her, she was next to him on the couch, touching his face and curling up against him. She was still like a kid, Rick thought, awed by him. Even though she had become more direct in speaking to him, she still lapsed into childhood, reaching back to the times when her only desire in life was to emulate him. She had followed him everywhere and had tried outdoing his friends in sports, raging when she fell short of her goals and they laughed benevolently at her zest for competition. But all that had passed, and with the years she had grown gracefully into womanhood, the driving spirit which was her trademark, transformed into her need to prove herself academically. She traveled nearly two hours each morning to attend Bronx High School of Science, something which she did for three years. Their parents at first had been worried but sensed that to attempt to dissuade her would break her spirit. The drive urged her to study and become a person to be reckoned with, a credit to their people, as their father had put it on numerous occasions. She spoke rapidly, excited at seeing Rick again, changing back and forth from English to Spanish, some sentences rising and falling with the peculiarity of rhythm which Yiddish gave English in Brooklyn. One might call it Bruklin Borincano, so that describing a history professor at school she once said: "*Ay no*, Ricky! I can't stand him. *Es tan antipático*. Such a schmuck!" Rick wondered if his father thought Christina was a silly woman.

"Oh, my God," she said, scrambling from the couch and rushing to her friend, whom she'd left standing by the door while she had been nuzzling him. "Elizabeth, this is my brother Rick." And taking the girl's hand she brought her forward. "Rick, this is Elizabeth Conde."

The girl said hello but avoided looking directly at him. She was one of those withdrawn, slowly maturing girls who looked as if they had never seen anything more serious than a minor traffic accident in which the drivers got calmly out of their cars, inspected the slight damage and exchanged insurance information. Elizabeth was a head taller than his sister, about the same Indian-tinted complexion. She was pretty but there seemed to be a veil of rules and regulations which she had accepted and which clouded her eyes with imposed innocence. Also notable in his assessment of Elizabeth Conde was the inoffensive plumpness which would eventually render her passive. She reminded him of some of his clients. Like his sister, Elizabeth was dressed in bell bottom trousers and platform shoes and newly applied purple lipstick. Rick smiled at her, feeling for a moment as if he was about to do an intake on someone at the settlement house. Christina asked Elizabeth to sit down. "Don't worry," she said. "He won't bite." She winked at Rick and told him Elizabeth was studying to be a teacher. "Early childhood education major," Christina said. "She's really great with kids." Turning to her friend, she informed her that Rick was a social worker on the Lower East Side.

"Really?" she said.

"Not really," he said, "but I'm working on it."

There had been no surprise in Elizabeth's voice. Rick was certain his sister had already given her a big buildup about him. The subject of his job was a touchy one, but he had never discussed it with Chris and there was no sense going into it now. He was not an MSW like Weintraub and his girlfriend Louise, or even Escobar with all his jargon and Irish wife.

"I'm taking classes at the New School at night. The settlement is paying the tuition," Rick had said. It was his defense against committing himself to the job. What the hell was he anyway? He had majored in Literature and Psychology and for a while had dabbled unsuccessfully in poetry. Goldstein, the director, had hired him to serve as a "buffer" between the staff and the neighborhood, on the promise that he'd pursue studies towards an MSW. Color him brown and *verde espéralo*, the color his father gave all that one had little chance of obtaining, in his own case, because he had seen the futility of working in the field. But at least going to school at night postponed his being branded with the idiotic letters. MSW stood for Master of Stupid Work.

Elizabeth smiled weakly and sat at the other end of the couch. "Do you work with children?" she asked, looking as if at any moment he'd ask her to leave the room and fill out a form that would give her license to speak without being spoken to.

"Sure," he said, still smiling patiently at her. "Families come in and we work with the whole unit." He hated the words, much as he hated "client," "low income," "economically deprived," "inner city," and "educationally handicapped." They were empty words, sounds devoid of meaning and, more insultingly, euphemisms for the multitude of problems and the horror which they produced in human beings.

"I bet it's interesting work," Elizabeth said. "Have you read Maria Montessori?"

Rick answered that it had been required reading for one of his courses in college and suppressed his amusement at Elizabeth's earnestness.

"Liz is our resident intellectual," Christina said. The remark made the girl blush deep purple. With the years she would be grotesque, Rick thought. His father was right, silly women were nothing but trouble. "I'm only kidding," Christina said, quickly. She rushed and sat between the two of them. "No, really, Rick," she said, turning to him. "Liz's going to be a terrific teacher. *Bien chévere.* She's got fantastic ideas about children."

"I'm sure she does," he answered.

"I'm not kidding, Rick," said Christina. "And she writes, too. I mean not poetry but essays and stuff. I kid around but I bet one of these days people are going to be using Liz's ideas. They make perfect sense. I mean, she believes children should be treated like princes and princesses during their formative years."

"What years?" Rick said, raising his eyebrows and squinting at his sister.

"I know, I know," she replied. "You don't like to hear jargon, but I think it makes sense."

Rick nodded patiently and wondered what the hell had gotten into his sister. She was definitely pushing Elizabeth on him. Maybe his father was right and they had already conspired to marry him off to her. Princes and princesses? All of a sudden his mind snapped and he saw the joke inherent in Elizabeth. He wanted to share it with his sister but it would be petty and cruel. What was purple and ruled Early Childhood Education? Answer: Elizabeth the Grape. He smiled inwardly and decided to change the subject.

"And you, Chris," he said. "What are you going to do? You thinking of becoming a teacher too?"

"Me? Das no my yob, men," answered his sister, affecting a Spanish accent and imitating the latest TV personality, one of their own who had apparently made it. She mimicked the comedian, rolling her eyes and shuffling a quick dance step after jumping up from the couch. Everyone laughed, including their father, who prided himself on speaking "good English." After the laughter died down Christina turned deadly serious. "I really don't know," she said. Her concern was genuine and Rick was touched. "I have another year before I have to decide on a major."

"What's your favorite course?" Rick asked, lapsing into his best counseling voice without feeling self-conscious.

"All of them except history and sociology."

"Out of all of them, which one really turns you on? That's really the question," he said.

"I don't know. Lit., Psych., Anthro. I'm even getting into Philosophy. Wait a minute, for a guy who doesn't like labels, you sure are hell bent on pinning one on me."

"Yeah, I guess you're right," he said, and wondered if her displeasure was part of her disappointment at his disinterest in Elizabeth. "Girls don't really have to be anything," he said, as if the question bored him. He was joking but Christina jumped back to the couch and not exactly playfully held her small fist to his face. He laughed and she slumped back on the couch, shaking her head.

"Boy, are you a class A chauvinist," she said. "Who would've thought it! My brother, the liberal, is really an MCP."

Their father had been sitting back, enjoying their quick give-and-take, but Rick's words made him sit up and offer his opinion. "Rick's right," he said. "It's okay for a girl to go to school but she should also think about setting up a home."

"Oh, Pop," Christina said, rising dejectedly from the couch.

"Don't start that again, okay?"

"No, it's true," he answered. "Look at your sister. She got her degree and is raising a family, too. In a few years, when the kids are a little bigger, she can get her license and teach."

"C'mon," said Christina. "Becky'll be tied to those kids until she's gray."

Their father laughed and slapped his knee.

"She's something, ain't she, Rick?" he said, looking to him for support.

"Go ahead and laugh," Chris said, defiantly. "This is one *corazoncito lindo* who's not getting caught up in all that marriage-house-children baloney." Their father stopped laughing and a hurt look appeared on his face. Chris, however, had no intentions of allowing herself to be manipulated into silence. "No, really, I mean it. That's all we're programmed for. One generation after the other. From house to school to church and back to the house. Engagement, marriage and babies. We might as well be a bunch of hicks. Look at Rick. You think he'd be married by now, right? Wrong! He knows better. Why do you think he only takes out American girls?" When Chris got going, thought Rick, she was merciless. Regardless of consequences, anything which bolstered her argument was employed. One thing was certain, she wasn't pushing Elizabeth at him for the purposes of hooking him up. Realizing that perhaps his sister was honestly trying to expose her friend to the world she enjoyed through him made him feel guilty that he'd been so thoughtless. Chris had now moved to the middle of the living room and was all of a sudden the street-wise tomboy who'd known little fear growing up. She was up on her toes, her head turned arrogantly to the side and her right index finger stabbing down to make her point. And yet the pose was innocent, devoid of any malice, the words lacking in venom. Nevertheless, Rick was annoyed that she'd brought up the subject of his preference for American girls. It seemed impossible she had forgotten the last scene with his father. To spite him he had begun toying with the idea of marrying Kathy Bauer. He had talked generally around the subject, testing Kathy but in effect teasing her with the possibility. She had waited patiently, accepting the change in him. After a while, feeling deceived, she moved out and in time was gone out of his life, another in a string of broken white hearts, he later thought in false self-deprecation.

"I'm telling you," Chris said, to no one. "I'm not going to stand around and let it happen to me. I'll kill myself first."

"That's enough, Chris," Rick said, suddenly. As if she had been slapped, the tone of his voice made her recoil, her theatrical arrogance shattered. She held back her tears and shook her head, not quite believing his betrayal. She quickly regained control but the hurt in her voice made the words mockingly bitter and filled with vengeance.

"Oh, Rick, not you too," she said, smiling pityingly at him. "You know what I'm saying is true. You're scared too. You know that."

"Why don't you try to relax, Chris," he said, already regretting that he had not been able to see her need for his support. They were both in the same boat and he should have known better. "I'm sorry, I really am," he said. But she was beyond the point at which she could accept his apology and went on.

"Who was the last P.R. you went out with?" she said. "Margie Betancourt, right? In your last year of high school, right? You met her at that camp you worked at as a counselor. She was from the Bronx, wasn't she? And she wasn't any little hick, was she? She had her thing together. Getting ready to go to City College, hip, articulate, pretty and proud, honey. It scared you, didn't it? You knew she meant business from the giddyup. Maybe she didn't want to get married right away but she wasn't into no light romance, either. I almost didn't recognize her. That's right, she's at Hunter. Not because she had changed or nothing. She's still pretty and hip, but because she's got a Ph.D. in Math and her name is Professor Margaret Betancourt Draper. That's right, she just got married last year. Some WASP M.I.T. genius. But back then she saw something in you and you couldn't be bothered. Am I right?"

Rick answered that she was right, that he had no defense against her argument. He looked to Elizabeth, seeking neutral ground. She had shrunk to child-size and, fearing involvement in the turmoil, stared blankly at the wall behind him.

"Rick has to get established first," their father said, as if it behooved him to defend the male point of view. "He has to take care of his studies. The economy isn't what it used to be. Look at Ralph. He and Becky got another kid coming and his salary isn't gonna be enough to support the four of them. He's gonna have to risk his life eight hours a day fighting crime in Harlem and then find himself something else on the side, moonlighting."

"Good for him," Chris snapped. "Serves them both right. If you want to dance, you gotta pay the piper."

Whether their father misunderstood the phrase was not clearly apparent to Rick, but he imagined the saying being lost in translation, possibly inferring sexual connotations and making the matter of the piper, somehow, obscene to him.

"I'm gonna pretend I didn't hear that," he said. "One thing I'm not gonna stand for in my house is that kind of talk, especially about your own sister."

Vanquished, her argument useless, Chris stood up in the middle of the floor, biting her lip and looking down at her feet. Their mother, who had been listening to the argument, gauging the tones of the voices as they shifted from the usual bantering to more heated words, called Chris into the kitchen. Rick imagined that once in there she would be reminded of their father's condition. Chris turned and motioned Elizabeth to follow, but the girl shook her head and said she had to return downstairs and help her mother. When the door was closed, Chris came back through the living room, her head still down, avoiding Rick's eyes and those of their father. She disappeared behind the wall which served to separate living room and kitchen in housing projects all over the city, reappearing periodically as she went about setting the table. Rick tried to reassure their father that Chris hadn't meant anything by her words.

"People say crazy things when they're worried," he said.

"I understand," said his father.

"It's just an American saying."

"Yeah, I know, Ricky," his father replied. "I know what she's talking about. I know she didn't mean no harm."

Rick was certain that his father still didn't understand and that under some highly complex pretext he would take the train to South Brooklyn to see his buddy, Angelo, at work and ask him, again in some convoluted way so that his ignorance remained hidden, about paying the piper. What pride! He was the man, the head of the family, and under no circumstance should he appear weak to any of its members. And yet he was wise in his own way. If he found nothing amiss with the saying, within a week it would be part of his repertoire of clichés and Chris would know that everything was all right between them.

*   *   *

The rest of the evening went as well as could be expected. Before their mother called them to eat, Chris returned to the living room and apologized to their father. She sat on the arm of his chair and smoothed his hair, not saying anything until he put an arm around her. When he did so she slid to his lap and cried and said she was going to be good and not to worry. "I know, baby," he said, holding her like he had held all his children when they were afraid or lonely, allowing his heart to expand to take them in. Rick felt a twinge of jealousy as he watched Chris bury her face in their father's shoulder, but he could not identify the source of his feelings other than to ascribe them to that all encompassing category labeled "sibling rivalry."

As always, the food was delicious. As if their mother possessed a deeper instinct, the pork was extremely lean and very little shortening had been used on the *tostones*. Rick found himself savoring every bit of his mother's cooking, relishing the taste of the red beans as they mixed with white rice in his mouth. As they ate they talked about the food, comparing how it stacked up against other cuisine, Latin or otherwise. Their mother urged everyone to have seconds, which she always did as a matter of course, lamenting how thin everyone was and how everything would be left if they didn't eat. When everyone had again heaped their plates, the conversation turned away from food and the present, to the past, the words weaving in and out of celebrated Christmases, birthdays, baptisms, Easters, vacations, both of their parents recalling anecdotes about him and Chris. Listening to his father, Rick tried recalling his father making a kite for him when he was seven but could not.

"We used to live near Prospect Park," his father said, urging him to remember. "I made it right in the apartment. On the island we used to make them out of bamboo and I found this old bamboo chair down on the docks and brought it home and bought some colored paper. *Papel de seda*, we used to call it back home. Silk paper, you know. It was green and yellow. A big box kite. You remember, Ricky!"

"I think so," he said, but couldn't remember.

His father's manner had become totally open, vulnerable, as he recalled those days. He turned to their mother. "You should've seen us, Margarita. Everybody had those store bought kites. It was in the spring. April or May, and there was a lot of wind. A weekend. Saturday morning and here we came, me and Ricky with our monster kite with the long ten foot tail made out of strings and *trapos*. Rag strips that I tore up from one of your old slips, Margarita. People stood around watching us like we was crazy. Some kids even said the kite wouldn't fly because it was too big." He now turned to Rick. "'You just watch,' I said to them. Rick, I gave you the kite and told you to walk away from me and I began unwinding the string and you kept going back until you was the size of my pinky you was so small. And then I started running and told you to let go. I could feel the string getting tight in my hands but I didn't look back until I could feel the kite take off. When I stopped running it was way up in the air like a big green and yellow bird, a dragon maybe, with its tail waving in the wind. You came running to me and I let you hold it and we let it fly for about three hours. Half a mile up in the air and it still looked like a building, it was so big. Three hours." He laughed now. "We got hungry but luckily there was a big crowd watching us and a hot dog man came over and we bought two of them. You didn't like sauerkraut in those days," he said, winking knowingly at him. Neither Chris nor their mother understood their private joke and he smiled sadly at his father's attempt at manly camaraderie. "Pretty soon people start asking all kinda questions about where I bought the kite and how much it cost. I laughed and told them I could make kites that looked like airplanes, cars, boats, birds, fish and anything else they could think of. The kids stood there with their mouths open, their little blue eyes asking more questions but not saying anything. You remember now, don't you, Rick?"

"Sure, Pop, now I remember," he said, but still felt the emptiness where the kite should've been. "It's just that I was small."

"Sure, I understand. It was beautiful. After a while we took down the kite. People still couldn't believe how such a big thing could stay up in the air. On the way home through the park it started to rain. We ran as fast as we could but by the time we got home all the silk paper was messed up and ripped and you cried."

His father was silent then, sensing that perhaps Rick could not recall the incident. Chris broke the silence by suggesting that their father make kites again.

"Boy, I bet they'd sell like crazy. It's not just a kid thing anymore. Everybody flies them. You know, custom-made kites. People pay good money for stuff like that. You should go to F.A.O. Schwartz and see the prices for really junky stuff, Pop. Wow, you could work right here in the house. Plenty of people do that now. You could use Rick's room. Right, Ricky?"

"Sure, Pop," he said, halfheartedly.

It had been the wrong thing to say but he was caught. If he disagreed he would hurt Chris. But with his agreeing, all his father could feel was that Rick didn't understand him. He watched his father's face grow troubled as he was reminded that he could no longer work at what he loved and worse, he'd have to work alone in the house, like a woman.

"No," he said, mournfully. "I mean, I think it's a good idea but I couldn't make things like that for money. That's not work. It's like playing the guitar or something. You make a kite like that and it's like having a kid. You take it out and let it fly and hope the string doesn't break and you lose it. And then you bring it home and put it in a safe place and if there's a little rip you fix it and check the tail to make sure it isn't ripped up. And each day you look at it until you bring it out and fly it again. Selling it would be like letting your own kid go live with somebody else. You know that, Rick. You have to see it everyday."

Rick did not answer. All at once his father looked very old, defeated, done in by the pace he had kept up all those years of slaving away to have a good life. The meal had been over more than twenty minutes and all at once the apartment was very quiet. Rick could hear the whirring of the refrigerator's motor and the electric clock making the curious vibrating sound each time the second hand went past the eight. His father got up from the table, went into the living room and turned on the television set. Chris and his mother slowly began clearing the table and Rick walked over and sat on the couch. Everything had become clouded and he wasn't sure if the kite incident had taken place or if his father had invented it. He sat, letting his mind relax, not wanting to say anything, hoping it would come to him.

When Chris and their mother were finished in the kitchen they came in and sat down but still no one would say anything. After some time, Rick looked at his watch, got up and went over to his father. "I have to leave now, Pop," he said. His father got up and after Rick kissed his mother and Chris, promising to see them again soon, his father walked him out of the apartment and down the hall to the elevator. The distance, the respect, was still there between them but they both knew Rick had no recollection of the kite. They put their arms stiffly around each other and said goodbye.

"Don't stay a stranger, Ricky," his father said when the elevator came. "You know, your mother worries about you," he added, self-consciously, aware that his son had finally seen through him, but that mentioning his mother was the only way he could express his own concern.

"Okay, Pop," Rick said. "Take care of yourself." He meant it so that in saying it he felt the ache his father also felt at the uncertainty of the future. "I'll see you soon." He rode the eleven flights down, feeling as if he had been on an extended roller coaster ride. It was always like that whenever he came over to see him. Even when everything went well between them, he felt as if he had gone back in time and was being asked to scrutinize every aspect of his life in the minutest detail.

*   *   *

The ride from the Coney Island terminal into Manhattan on the "D" train was usually a tiresome, sleep-inducing trip. At ten o'clock at night, the express had stopped running and each station was nearly deserted. People on the train seemed, each one, to be feigning sleep. It was a New York way of being wary while at the same time relaxing so that if one were a mugger, a molester or a pickpocket, one would have to decide whether the person was in fact off guard or playing at it. He had gotten this information from one of his clients' son, who, at fourteen, was already a chronic thief. It was a silly game, playing possum. In spite of precautions, things always happened when one least expected them. When he boarded the train, Rick found himself a twin seat at the end of the car, opened a book he had begun reading the previous night and let the words carry him to the time of slavery in Cuba. *La Historia de un Cimarrón*, he had decided, was a propaganda tract and anybody with half a brain could see through it. He had no quarrel with its purpose and as a matter of fact found it fascinating. Beyond that, however, he enjoyed his ability to let the Spanish language flow through him without his having to translate into English and back again as had happened for a time. The problem had caused him some anguish and kept him forever asking himself why he had to exist between two languages. As the doors opened and he looked up to check on the new passengers, he saw a young woman enter the car, then seat herself directly across from him.

She was attractive, Latin, New York, hard. Something else compelled him to look at her more closely. The girl appeared to be on her way to something quite special and yet he immediately felt as if that event or place for which she was headed existed solely in her mind. As soon as the train doors closed, she began grooming herself, unconsciously, resembling, but lacking the grace and fluidity of an animal. Her large brown eyes seemed empty, her awareness detached, as she brushed her long hair, dyed a deep auburn. After some five minutes she replaced the brush with a pocket mirror and began examining her face. Although made up rather heavily, she again applied lipstick to her mouth and then proceeded to remove her eyelashes. With great ceremony she replaced them with a more luxuriant pair, which, adding to the vacuousness of her eyes, gave her a perfect, babydoll-like appearance.

So precise and intense was her concern with her looks that Rick thought she might be a male. He looked closely at her face but found no traces of masculinity. She was not a male but neither was she a female. He tried returning to the book, could not concentrate and looked around the train to see if anyone else had noticed the strange young woman. The car had filled up considerably as it approached the heart of Brooklyn. The passengers, however, appeared oblivious to everything but their "Night Owl" edition of the *Daily News*, or their own thoughts, the steady clacking of wheel against rail serving as a hypnotic instrument to their lethargy. Only the warning bell which preceded the closing doors on the new train activated them and in unison they bobbed their heads to the two tone warning.

Only one person seemed conscious of the drama being played out between himself as an observer, and the image of humanity across the aisle. For, Rick Sánchez thought, if the young woman's compulsiveness could have been called insanity, then surely it was nothing more than an exaggerated pantomime of life and the quiet pretense under which humans labored, forever toiling towards no apparent end, knowing only they were traveling with increasing rapidity in the same direction but busying themselves with whatever role each had been assigned. The other observer with whom Rick felt immediate kinship was another young woman. She was wearing a long green coat, knitted green hat, matching gloves. *Verde que te quiero verde*, he thought, recalling García Lorca's poem. She was what Rick had learned to classify as a good, goodlooking girl. He looked at her, back to the glamour queen and back again. She understood and smiled, almost with compassion, as if in finding the scene tragic, she could nevertheless share in its absurdity.

For the moment, he was thankful that someone was not afraid to share this knowledge. He tried returning to the book but found himself looking up again. This time his gaze went directly to the girl in green. Without a trace of reserve she smiled openly at him. It was the sort of smile one gets from a person with whom something of value has been shared, a mutually discovered secret. A love smile, he thought. Not sexual love but love founded on trust. The thought disturbed him immensely. She continued to smile. It was a game and she was an expert, never letting the smile come at him from the same angle. Whereas the other girl had drawn attention to herself by heavy and repetitious movement, this one tilted her head slightly, or else raised it, one time smiling fully, the next, the smile barely on her lips but slowly filling her eyes as if the mixture of joy and mirth were a delicately blended liquid which rose from mouth to eyes by means of valvular manipulation. He imagined an exotic, green and cream-colored tropical fish, rising and falling in the deep blue water. She was a child, he thought, like his sister, full of ideals and romance. His admiration for her turned to pure lust and he imagined her naked beneath him, realizing almost immediately how resentful he had grown of the innocence of others in the past year.

As the train neared Atlantic Avenue, the girl stood up and approached the door near him. She was saying goodbye, smiling, her eyes still playful. She carried books and a light tan bag, the smooth leather matching her delicate complexion. He smiled and only when the doors opened and she was out of the train did he realize he would never see her again. As the warning bells went off, he followed her out just managing to avoid the closing doors. Not knowing what he was to say, he raced after her. Once he made sure she was not transferring to another train, he slowed down his pace. "That was something, wasn't it?" he said, as he caught up to her. It was as if she had been expecting him to follow her. She nodded, smiled, her teeth very small and even. He was now walking beside her and a faint trace of an exquisite fragrance heightened his awareness of her. He had never seen a face like hers. Never. The skin was very clear and smooth and pulled tight to her cheekbones, causing her eyes to appear deeper, greener.

"I see her almost every night on my way home," she said.

"You're kidding!"

"It's true. I think she's a topless dancer or something. Sometimes she looks like she's rehearsing and she moves her shoulders to the beat of the train."

He loved her voice. It had a strange, reedy quality, much as if she were playing an instrument. They had walked through the tunnel, the turnstile, up the stairs and out into the night. The street was deserted, the icy wind blowing papers in crazy whorls across the cobblestone. Only the man at the newspaper stand, clapping his hands, clad in fingerless gloves, destroyed Rick's feeling that Brooklyn had been evacuated and he and the girl were the only ones left.

"Do you go to school?" he asked, buttoning his overcoat against the cold.

"Yes."

"Evening school?"

"Sort of. Nursing school."

"Aren't you afraid coming home so late at night?" She shook her head and laughed. "I take karate lessons on Tuesday and I carry a long letter opener." She stopped walking and took the weapon out of her handbag. The word "Toledo" had been inscribed on the blade of the tiny sword. "I took it from an Iberia office in Manhattan."

"The airline?"

"Yeah," she said, and laughed again. "I boost things. I'm real dangerous, so watch it," she added, taking back the letter opener. She resumed walking and about halfway down the block stopped under the streetlight, looking up at him, her face still open, smiling, her cheeks already reddened by the cold. All at once he felt foolish. Never at a loss for words with women, he'd been silenced by her. "I have to wait for my bus," she said.

"Can I walk you home?" he asked, feeling as if he were back in high school. She shrugged her shoulders and said she'd be all right.

"I have to take the bus. It leaves me a block from the house. You can wait here with me if you want. Sometimes it takes forever."

"How about a cup of coffee, then?"

She acquiesced, returning the offer with a smile in her eyes.

"What's your name?" she asked once they were seated in a booth in a dingy coffee shop. When he told her, she said, "My name's Lolín. María Dolores Pacheco to be exact."

"You're Spanish?" he said, incredulously. What an idiot he was. All the clues had been there. The way she smiled, her sureness, the way she used the word "boost." She was now shaking her head at him disapprovingly.

"Puerto Rican," she said. "What did you think I was?" And then she lapsed into street Spanish. "*¡Adiós, mira éste! ¿Qué es lo tuyo, m'ijo?* Dig him! *¡Parejero!* You mean you couldn't tell?"

"No, I thought you were Italian or something."

"Italian?"

"Yeah!"

"You're kidding. *¡Qué arrebate, m'ijo!* Italian?"

"Yeah, or I thought maybe you were from the Middle East when you got off at Atlantic. You know, Armenian or Lebanese. You know, your eyes, they're almond shaped."

"What does that mean!"

"It's supposed to be a sign of beauty."

"I bet," she replied, not quite believing him.

She had him coming and going, tongue-tied half the time and the other half staring dumbly at her face. She had taken off her hat, revealing loosely curled, shiny black hair which framed her face and made her twice as alluring. He couldn't recall how long they sat in the diner, smiling mostly and talking nonsense about high school stories, movies, clothes, and the topless dancer. They exchanged ages. She was twenty and when he told her his age she called him a *viejo*, and then amended it to "experienced," at which point he looked her in the eye and she blushed slightly. It was the first time he'd had the upper hand. At a quarter to twelve they decided it had grown late and walked back to the bus stop. When they were on the bus she sat next to him, still mischievous, arguing with him but without any of the sarcasm she had first displayed, her face glowing with excitement.

"I'm sorry," he said at one point. "I was reading and thinking about that girl. You know, trying to figure out what was the matter with her."

"Sorry about what?" she said.

"Mistaking you for an Armenian."

"Listen, I forgive you," she said, laughing and moving closer to him, not caring that their bodies touched. "But it's the last time you look at foreign girls."

He laughed, embarrassed by her aggressiveness, still not knowing when she was serious, but convinced now that she had been. He could feel all of her. Through the heavy clothing he felt her body and all of him grew warm and pleasant. The air felt charged with her and everything had become dreamlike.

"You don't live in Brooklyn, do you?"

"No, I couldn't help it," he said. "Getting off the train, I mean. I would've never seen you again."

"I know," she said. "I felt sort of sad, but that's New York. I'm used to it."

"You're not sad anymore, are you?"

"No, just tired," she said, and without warning, rested her head on his shoulder. "I feel like I've just finished running. Do you like to dance?" He said he did and she asked if he'd take her.

"I hear about those places but I've never been. I can't even imagine what it's like when people tell me about it. Not for nothing but I'm a real hick. A regular *marintaiga*." The word sent a shudder through him and memories of his childhood came flooding into his mind. He hadn't heard the word in years. And she'd used it as if she heard it every day. She had been born and raised in New York but was still a *marintaiga*. *La mancha de plátano*, his mother called it. Once you were stained by the plantain, thus you remained, indelibly branded for life, generation upon generation. "You'll take me, won't you?" she pleaded, sleepily. "My mother's so strict but she'll let me go with you when she finds out you're a college graduate and everything. She's so old fashioned. It's just me and her and my grandmother and I don't feel like hurting them. They're angels, really. Mami just works and saves her money to buy a little house in P.R. for her and *abuela*. They both worry I'm going to end up like Mami. You know, pregnant and without a man. Are you political?" He asked her what she meant and she explained. "I started going to these discussion meetings and I'm reading about P.R. and what's happened down there. I don't read Spanish well, but I force myself if I have to. I want to know everything about the island. You know, the history and the culture. What I said about boosting is silly. It doesn't make any sense and I'm not going to do it anymore. I mean, they did steal a lot from us. First the Spanish and then the Americans."

He explained that he wasn't very political. "I believe in independence for Puerto Rico," he said, although he wasn't sure what he really meant in saying it.

"Would you live there? If it was independent?"

He couldn't answer her, unable to understand the significance of the question, and finally said he didn't know. She said she didn't know either. She didn't push the issue. Automatically, her hand went up to the cord to signal the driver.

*   *   *

The next few minutes were like a nightmare. One second she was holding on to his arm, then she was clutching it. Her books lay scattered on the sidewalk. As the bus pulled away she let go of his arm and ran down the street and around the corner. It was then that he smelled the smoke and heard the rush of water from the hoses and the pumper's engine. He picked up the books and raced around the corner after her.

Across the street, along a row of old frame houses, a wall of flames rose against the night sky, lighting up the entire block as if one were looking at it through red cellophane. The water from the fire fighting equipment hit futilely at the wind-swept flames and, like dancing demons, enormously angry at being disturbed, the columns of fire exploded upwards, sending a shower of sparks forward into the street and into the firemen aiming the hoses. People gasped at the sight and he felt a blast of heat hit his face. Not sure what to make of it, Rick began looking for Lolín.

He finally found her at the other end of the block. She was being held back by two policemen. In the confusion of her flight she'd lost her hat and her purse and was fighting the two cops, her voice already hoarse. He managed to disentangle her from the two officers, explaining that he was a friend. At first she didn't recognize him and fought him with the same intensity she'd directed at the police. All around them voices explained that it had been a flash fire, electrical or something. He held her, talking all the while until she went limp and all the fight left her. And then as if she once more realized the extent of the fire, she was digging her fingernails into his arm, her hand becoming rigid and her face distorted by the knowledge that it was impossible for anyone to get out of the house alive. "Oh, my God," she kept saying, even when he held her to him, soothing her. "Oh, my God. Oh, Mami. What am I going to do?"

When the fire was finally brought under control an hour later and the morgue wagon came to take away the two bodies, he remained with her, riding in the police car, holding her books and hat while she clutched her wet pocketbook to herself, staying with her throughout the long night and the identification of the charred bodies and the questions, crying with her and feeling her pain and her loss, smoothing her hair, caressing her face, ravaged now by the tragedy, the light in her eyes nearly dimmed as she fought to accept that her mother and grandmother were gone forever.

"What am I going to do, Ricky?" she asked, momentarily lucid. He had not been able to answer her and once again, as if the fire had suddenly touched her, she shuddered and screamed. Wailing, keening, her pain came in long, shrill cries, and cut deep into him and left him raw; his father's own impending death was dwarfed by her sorrow. He told her over and over that he would take care of her somehow. The words were coming without any control on his part calling her *mamita*, like she was his own flesh and blood, joined, nay, fused, wedded many years before, and the knowledge, stored in his mind, coming slowly alive.

By five that morning they had left the morgue and he managed to get her back to his apartment. He made her drink warm milk and cinnamon, laced with a shot of whiskey and made her lie down. He wasn't able to sleep and every couple of minutes he got up out of the couch to look in on her in the bedroom. When she finally fell asleep and her face began to gain some semblance of tranquility, he dozed off. Towards sunrise he was up again. He looked out the window and watched the light of the new day, the water of the East River like a silver mirror and the bridges to Brooklyn faintly drawn in the winter mist.

At eight o'clock he phoned his parents' home, knowing his mother would be up preparing breakfast for Chris. Chris answered the phone and he explained briefly what had happened.

"Is Pop awake yet?" he said.

"Yes, he's up. Do you want me to tell him?"

"That's all right, Chris. Let me talk to him." He waited, and when his father came to the phone, he said, "I need your help, Papi," dropping the English "Pop" for the more tender name he had used for addressing him in his childhood.

"Anything, Ricky," said his father.

He explained the situation and then waited in the apartment until his father and mother came to stay with Lolín. His mother touched Lolín's cheek as soon as she saw her and then held her when she began crying again, talking to her in Spanish and crying with her as if they had known each other before and the girl's loss was her own. His father wasn't able to look at him directly, his eyes averted as if to guard against breaking down and crying, maintaining even then the stoic pose, nodding philosophically and telling him he had always known Rick had a good heart and that he would have done the same thing.

*   *   *

Now, as he sat at his desk drinking hurriedly-bought coffee, Rick Sánchez once again pondered the events of the previous day. His head ached. The two hours of sleep he had managed would not be enough to see him through the day. More than ever he wished his job were simple. Before too long, an avalanche of distraught mothers would descend on his office to demand an explanation for not being able to obtain food stamps or why their rent had been increased. Referring them to the proper agencies had proven useless. Invariably, people came back with renewed bitterness and a longer list of complaints, their pride restraining the desperation of years of futile struggle, created, Rick had decided, by their own ignorance and inflexibility, they sought solace in him.

But it wasn't just them. It was everything. The settlement house was a testing ground, a laboratory in which chronically neurotic "professionals" examined the exquisite form human misery took among the "new immigrants." Another of their favorite phrases. Later that morning there would be a meeting with Goldstein and the rest of the staff to plan the children's Christmas party. In well-meaning but condescending language, Goldstein would explain the importance of the season to the Puerto Rican family, while VISTA volunteers, full-fledged social workers, psychologists, family planners and the rest of the vultures who daily picked over the bones of a culture in its death throes, asked their usual silly, middle class questions about themes and communication. It was their own personal sociology seminar, created through some obscure process to offer relief for their guilt.

Rick stood up, opened the file cabinet behind his desk and extracted several files. After a few minutes of staring at them on his desk he pushed them away. It was useless. As if the upcoming problems of the day weren't enough, he now had Lolín to worry about. Although he recoiled from the horror of the previous night, he felt drawn to it, hoping that within the series of events leading up to the tragedy, there was a way out, some minute and seemingly unimportant detail which would absolve him of culpability. Perhaps if he hadn't insisted that Lolín come with him to the diner she would've arrived on time to save her mother and grandmother. Then again, he thought, she may have perished with them.

The thought produced horror in him as he recalled the limp, body bags being removed from the smoldering skeleton of the house and placed in the morgue wagon. He was jarred away from the image by the ringing of the telephone. It was Mrs. Thomas, Goldstein's secretary. She wanted to know if there were any last minute items which he wanted included in the agenda for that afternoon's meeting. He said he had nothing but that she shouldn't forget his item about the need for a drug orientation clinic. Mrs. Thomas made an oblique statement about the resistance his suggestion had met at the last meeting. On the verge of screaming, Rick insisted. He hung up the phone, tried to become interested once more in the files but again met with failure.

Suddenly, the nearly empty coffee container he brought to his lips became the object of his wrath and in controlled anger, wishing more to hurl it against the postered walls or crush it in his hand, he placed it in the trash can next to his desk. The throbbing behind his eyes had become more intense in the past half hour and he wished he had remained home. He could've called in sick but he suffered from the same guilt which assailed the others. At some point he had passed through that magic door which transformed ordinary human beings into Americans and, having done so, he now had to carry a similar burden. Excuses were not part of the intake process. And yet, if he had to make excuses he could have, having listened to them each day for the past two years. No matter how clearly neighborhood people were in the wrong, they always had an excuse.

His thoughts again turned to Lolín. Her grief, the outpouring of pain, was more than he had ever experienced, the loss so immense that he couldn't imagine how she'd bear it the rest of her life. And now he was part of it, his life and hers and his parents and the ones who each day came to him, intertwined. All of them were cast together like so many leaves blown by the wind, never knowing and yet suspecting, odious as the notion seemed to his otherwise clear and unsuperstitious mind, that destiny had played a part in bringing all of them together. The thought filled him with hatred and once again he felt trapped. The emotion choked him and he wished to run from it all. But he couldn't now. He was linked to Lolín, to her grief, to his parents and their ceaseless toiling. He must tell them.

Resolutely, going beyond his anger, he dialed his own number. The phone rang several times before his father answered it. The voice on the other end sounded strangely subdued, new, much as if in the hour which had transpired since he had left his apartment his father had undergone a transformation.

"Pop?"

"Yes, Rick."

"You all right?"

"Sure, son. What's the matter?"

"Nothing. I just wanted to know how Lolín was doing."

"She's okay, Rick. Your mother fixed her some breakfast and she ate. We're getting ready to go back to Brooklyn. Ralph and Becky just got here with the car."

"Thanks, Pop."

"She says she doesn't have any other family," his father said, sadly.

"Yeah, I know."

"She can live with us if you want. I mean, until she can get herself a place."

"I'd like that, Pop. Let her have my room."

"Sure, Rick. It's a good room. It's got plenty of light and you can see the ocean from the window."

"Yes, Pop, it's a beautiful room," he said, and all at once he felt very tired as he remembered it all and was again in Prospect Park with his father, flying the kite against the brilliant spring sky.

"She's a very serious girl, Rick," said his father.

"I know, Pop," Rick answered, smiling at his concern for him.

"You and Mami take care of her until I'm ready. I'll see you tonight."

He hung up the phone. The tiredness was being replaced by a languorous feeling and once more he recalled the kite and why it had faded from his memory. His father and mother had quarreled, and his mother had cried. It was the first time he'd seen her cry and he hated his father for it. Even after the two of them made up and things had gone back to their usual pace, he had found it difficult to talk to his father. The kite had been a peace offering from him. Now, in his mind's eye, Rick saw Lolín's face clearly once again, her beautiful smile and playful eyes filling him so that a strange new power invaded his body, making his skin tingle. He felt his own smile come from deep within him, hurting the muscles of his jaw as if they hadn't been used in years.

He opened the top drawer of his desk and from it took out a pad of yellow paper. On it he began drafting a letter to Goldstein, explaining why he had to resign. He saw his task clearly now. Although he felt sympathy for the suffering in the neighborhood, he had to go beyond the daily routine of putting people's lives in order, if not for them, at least for their children. Somehow he had to find a way of letting them know what he saw and in so doing, show with his effort that not all of life was despair. When he finished writing the letter he walked down the hall to the Social Work secretary's office and had her type it.

Returning to his own office he once again sat at his desk, picked up his pen and in block letters, in the middle of the yellow pad, he wrote:

THE MARINTAIGA KITE

by

Rick Sánchez

It was a monster kite, blue and yellow, its tail like a comet against the blazing April sky . . .